Lincoln

COMMUNITIES, CULTURAL SERVICES
and ADULT EDUCATION
**This book should be returned on or before
the last date shown below.**

YESTERDAY'S CHILD

For ten long years Laura had cared for her sick mother. But then, when her mother died, she was alone in the world. Now in her mid-twenties, she begins to realise what she's missed out on during those important formative years. She's determined to make up for lost time: a career will be hers, as well as friends, a social life . . . and love. Yesterday's Child is going to become Today's Woman. But the journey will not be without its pitfalls . . .

JANET WHITEHEAD

YESTERDAY'S CHILD

Complete and Unabridged

LINFORD
Leicester

First published in Great Britain in 2008

First Linford Edition
published 2009

British Library CIP Data

Whitehead, Janet
    Yesterday's child.—Large print ed.—
    Linford romance library
    1. Love stories
    2. Large type books
    I. Title
    823.9′2 [F]

    ISBN 978–1–84782–607–7

Published by
F. A. Thorpe (Publishing)
Anstey, Leicestershire

Set by Words & Graphics Ltd.
Anstey, Leicestershire
Printed and bound in Great Britain by
T. J. International Ltd., Padstow, Cornwall

This book is printed on acid-free paper

This is for Angel Collins,
who is fast becoming
a very titled lady!

1

Had the day of Mrs Jennings' funeral been a scene from a book or a film, the weather would most probably have been dreadful. Dark storm clouds would have boiled up to blot out the sun, and torrential rain would have ensured that the graveside ceremony was both brief and wretched.

But as it was, that July day was actually very fine, with calm blue skies and pleasant temperatures, and that at least was a comfort to her daughter, Laura.

After the funeral, the three cars returned to the small Chiltern cottage in Larkfield Lane, where earlier Laura had prepared piles of ham and cheese sandwiches and a display of salad that seemed disgustingly colourful in the circumstances, and after what was deemed a respectable interlude, relatives and family friends began to eat and drink, to discuss Laura's mother and father and reminisce over 'the old days'.

Laura mingled constantly, making sure that no one went without, but she was still too numb to really make herself feel part of this group or the ritual for which it had gathered. She was in her own home, yes, among people she loved or felt warm attachments to, but she didn't feel that she *belonged*.

'Laura?'

The babble of conversation around her came back up to full volume, and as if waking from a dream, she realised that someone was standing directly in front of her in the comfortable living room, and that she had been asked a question. She blinked a few times, until her large hazel eyes focused on the young man who was studying her with such obvious concern.

'Are you all right, Laura?'

She took a deep breath and forced a smile. Mark Barber was one of the few people with whom she'd always felt comfortable. They'd known each other practically all their lives, since their fathers had been partners in a firm of local estate agents, a business that was still flourishing today, under Mark's watchful eye.

'I . . . I'm fine, thanks.'

'Well you don't *look* fine. Come and sit down for a minute.'

'I can't. I've got to — '

He raised a finger to silence her. 'You've spent your whole life looking after other people,' he reminded her. 'Now let someone else look after *you*.'

She allowed him to lead her across the room to a heavily stuffed sofa beneath an open bay window that looked out onto the lawn. An elderly aunt and uncle, engaged in conversation with some friends from the other side of the village, shifted up so that she could sit down. Mark knelt beside her.

'Now, what can I get you? A sandwich, maybe?'

'No, really. I — '

'Well at least let me get you a drink,' he said gently.

She allowed a fond smile to cross her otherwise troubled face. 'A glass of white wine, then,' she decided. 'A small one, mind.'

She watched him cross the room and disappear into the kitchen, where she'd left the wines and spirits on a tray by the sink for the guests to help themselves.

He was tall, and the cut of his black suit accentuated his naturally slim build. But even in childhood he'd been that way, she remembered. His playground nicknames had always included 'Lanky' and 'Tin-ribs'. But in twenty-six years he had grown to become a fine figure of a man, just as his father Derek must have been in *his* youth — although glancing at Derek now and finding him watching her from across the room with an expression she couldn't quite decipher, that seemed hard to believe.

Derek Barber looked at least a

decade older than his fifty-eight years. His hair was still thick and dark, but his skin was like parchment and his eyes were heavy-lidded and almost constantly bloodshot. A mild heart attack two years earlier had forced him to retire from the business, and since then he had grown increasingly belligerent. Now it was hard for Laura to imagine how she had ever come to regard this unsmiling, cantankerous man as far more than just an adopted uncle.

Her mood lightened a little when Mark reappeared in the kitchen doorway, a glass of wine in one hand and a sandwich on a plate in the other. When he was near enough, he handed her the drink and balanced the plate on the arm of the sofa.

'I know you're not hungry,' he said before she could protest, 'but it's there if you want it.'

'Thanks.'

Crouching beside her again, he glanced around the room, trying to think of a topic of conversation that would take her mind off things. They had never been stuck for words before, not once in their lifetime's friendship. Even as children they had gotten along famously. But now he could not think of a single subject that wouldn't seem contrived or clumsy.

Eventually, to help him out, Laura said again, 'Thanks.'

He looked baffled. 'What for? A glass of wine and a ham sandwich?'

Her smile came more naturally this time, and chased some of the misery from her otherwise fair and attractive face. 'You *know* what for,' she said quietly. 'For helping out the way you have, making all the arrangements — '

'That's what family's for,' he said.

Before he could say more, however, they both heard his father call his name, and across his shoulder Laura saw Derek leaning forward in his seat, beckoning with one claw-like hand.

Mark, raising his lively blue eyes to heaven in an attempt to cheer her up, said, 'Be back in a minute.'

But as he approached his parents, his mother's expression told him that something was wrong.

Shirley Barber was a tall, blonde fifty year-old with a dancer's figure and finely chiselled features. With her natural poise, tact and intelligence, Mark had often wondered why she had chosen to limit herself to motherhood. These days, however, she spent much of her free time organising charity functions in and around the village, and she seemed happy with that.

'We'll be going in a little while,' she said when he was near enough. 'Your father's not feeling very well.'

Mark switched his gaze to his father, who was now sitting back in his chair, looking grey and tired. 'What is it, Dad?'

Derek's heavy-lidded eyes came to rest on his son. 'Just . . . just the usual.'

'Chest pains,' Shirley whispered worriedly.

'Do you think I should call a doctor?' asked Mark.

'No, no . . . I've taken a pill. It . . . it'll work off in a minute.'

'It's been a trying day,' Shirley explained. 'What with the funeral and everything.'

'Yes,' Mark agreed. 'Look, I'll make our apologies to Laura, and then get you straight back home.'

For the first time Derek's sober face seemed to relax. 'About time,' he wheezed sourly. 'I never did care much for funerals.'

* * *

Twenty minutes later, Mark brought his silver-grey Hyundai Sonata to a gentle halt at the mouth of the gravel drive leading up to his parents' home, then turned in his seat to study his father.

'How do you feel now, Dad?'

'Better.'

'Are you coming in for a while?' asked his mother.

Mark shook his head. 'No, I'll go back to Larkfield Lane. I think Laura

8

needs all the support she can get at the moment.'

Derek snorted. 'Leave the girl to stand on her own two feet for a change,' he grumbled. 'God knows, it's about time.'

'Derek!' said Shirley.

'In any case,' he went on, ignoring her, 'you've got better things you could be doing, Mark. Barber and Jennings doesn't run itself, you know.'

Mark waited while his parents got out of the car, watching his father's slow, laboured movements through troubled eyes.

He found the change that had taken place in the older man during the past couple of years unsettling. Derek had always been a charming man: smart, upright, genial. As an estate agent he had been second to none, had developed the hard-but-subtle sell into a fine art. But it seemed to Mark that forced retirement might be causing him more harm than good.

Derek Barber wasn't cut out for a life

of ease. He thrived on business, which was why he and Robert Jennings had made such a success of their agency. Now there were five branches of Barber & Jennings spread throughout the county, and further expansion seemed highly likely over the next few years.

Seeing his parents turn back to face him, Mark waved, then sat there a moment longer, watching them walk up the drive to their elegant Regency-style house.

He could easily appreciate how his father must feel, having been relegated to the side-lines by ill-health. But instead of finding a new interest or hobby to occupy his spare moments, he seemed to have grown too bitter to care about anything, one way or the other.

Mark didn't like the direction his thoughts were taking. Though he hated to admit it, he was beginning to see a dark side to the man that he'd never thought existed.

★　★　★

As the events of the past few weeks finally began to hit home, Laura was seized by a sudden, fidgety restlessness, and hurriedly retreated into the garden.

At this time of year the garden was a riot of colour, with white alyssum, fuschia, geraniums and godetia forming a resplendent border between patio and lawn. Further back, at the head of the winding stone path, alpine plants stood sentry around the steps that led up to the rockery, pond and sun-loungers.

Wrapped up in her own thoughts, she failed to hear the first discreet cough behind her, then turned to find her Aunt Frances framed beneath the vine-strewn pergola, a faint smile quivering at her lips.

Aunt Frances was in her mid-sixties. She had a heart of gold and Laura loved her dearly. 'I wondered where you'd vanished to,' said the older woman. 'Are you all right, dear?'

'Fine. I just thought I . . . ' Laura shrugged. 'I wanted some fresh air.'

Her aunt came forward, and when

she stood face to face with Laura, studied her through melancholy eyes. Her own hair was as corngold as that of her niece, but arranged in a bun, while Laura's was cut in a neat, shoulder-length bob. They were of the same height, five and a half feet, and of a similar build, slim and compact. But there the similarities ended. For Aunt Frances had always been what she herself often referred to as a 'gay dog', while Laura was quiet, shy and introspective.

Without a word, she took Laura by the arm and led her up to the cool privacy of the rockery and pond, where they both sat on one of the sun-loungers.

'It's all right, Laura,' she said in a soft, understanding voice. 'You don't have to put on a show for me, you know. I understand exactly how you're feeling. I expect an interfering old aunt is the last thing you want around you at the moment. Am I right?'

'Of course not.'

Aunt Frances shook her head fondly. 'Good old Laura,' she said. 'Never one to complain.'

For a while they sat side by side in silence, feeling the warm breeze on their faces. Nearby, a line of ferns waved cheerily from side to side, like children who couldn't appreciate the gravity of the occasion.

'Would you like to talk about it, dear?' Aunt Frances asked quietly.

Laura shook her head, keeping her face pointed carefully away from the older woman.

'It might help, you know.'

'N — no. I don't think so.'

'I'll go back inside then, if you like. I mean, if you really *do* want to be alone. I shouldn't have disturbed you in the first place.'

A dragonfly landed on the surface of the pond, wrinkling it.

And then, suddenly, Laura could hold up no longer.

'Oh, Auntie — '

She seemed to melt into her aunt's

bony shoulder, and once there found solace in the warmth of her late father's only sister as she held her and patted her arm and made soft, comforting sounds.

A little while later, still cradling Laura in her arms, Aunt Frances stared off across the garden and beyond, her damp blue eyes distant. 'All this has left you in a pretty pickle, hasn't it?' she whispered.

Not trusting herself to speak, Laura only nodded.

But *a pretty pickle*, she thought, was putting it mildly. For her mother's death had raised some uncomfortable truths for Laura, truths she was reluctant to face.

Her mother had always been a weak, neurotic and — there could be no denying it — a selfish woman, more so after Laura's father had died. Then she had come to rely on Laura completely.

As a consequence, Laura had known little of life save her own blinkered routine of caring for her mother.

Not that she had ever regarded that as a chore. At least not at first. But towards the end — and especially in the last few years, when the woman within her began to fight to replace the girl — she had started to realise exactly how she had been manipulated and coaxed into committing herself to a mother who had never, *ever* encouraged her to lead a life of her own.

She felt a sharp stab of guilt, because she was at last facing the fact that her mother had never been the selfless saint she had always liked to imagine. In truth, Mrs Jennings had refused to allow her daughter to grow up in the natural way because it suited her better to have her as a constant, captive companion to help ease away some of her own loneliness.

Laura blamed herself for not realising it sooner. If she had, then perhaps she could have done something to get her mother to rekindle old friendships and take a more active part in life.

But the simple truth was that she

hadn't realised, and had been left by everyone save Aunt Frances to simply get on with it.

Glancing around the garden, across the ferns, hydrangea and lavender bushes without really seeing them, she tried to put the changes her mother's death had made into perspective.

All she had ever known was life here at the cottage. Even those happier times, when her father was alive, were now only distant memories. But it hadn't always been like that. Even as a shy child there had been so many things she had wanted to do — write, travel, find a career for herself the way Aunt Frances had, and eventually know the love of a good man and children . . .

But a percentage of the monthly profits from Barber & Jennings had provided a modest income, so there had never been any real need to find a job — even supposing her mother would have *allowed* her to — and as one year faded into another, she had fallen unsuspectingly into the trap of devoting

16

herself completely to her mother's care.

Completely.

And now that her mother had passed on . . . ?

She tried to fight back a new surge of hot, stinging tears, but couldn't stop one single, agonised sob from escaping as she realised the enormity of the answer to her question.

Now, she thought . . . *now there was nothing.*

2

Somehow, she survived the black spots of the next few days, knowing that if she allowed herself to think too deeply about the position in which she now found herself, she would be over-whelmed by despair.

It was better, she thought, to tackle her problem head-on.

The first thing she needed was a job. So she spent what seemed like hours going through the local paper, search-ing out vacancies she felt she might be suited to and then ringing or writing off for application forms. It made her feel good to be doing something positive at last.

Early one morning a few days later, just as she was sorting through her mother's effects, there was a ring at the door.

She hurried downstairs, past the

small reproduction heads of fishermen and Arabs on the wall, and along the neat, bright hallway, catching a glimpse of herself in the full-length mirror beside the telephone seat just before she reached the front door.

Today she was wearing a pale yellow blouse, a pair of casual light blue jeans and trainers. Her fine blonde hair was pulled back from her face in a pony-tail, accentuating the prominence of her high cheekbones and long, fashion-model's neck.

She opened the door to reveal a pretty young girl with wild auburn hair and an infectious grin. It was Karen Kingsley, the nineteen-year-old daughter of Clive and Mary Kingsley, her next-door neighbours.

'Hello! Not interrupting anything, am I?'

'No, not at all. How are you?'

'Oh, fine, thanks.'

The teenager made no move to continue the conversation, so Laura asked, 'How can I help you?'

Karen's grin grew wider. 'Well, it's more a case of how I can help *you*.'

'That sounds very mysterious.'

'It wasn't meant to. Can I come in for a bit? If you're sure I'm really *not* interrupting anything, that is?'

'Of course.'

She stood back to allow the younger girl entrance, then closed the door after her and ushered Karen into the living room.

'Can I get you something to drink?'

'Ooh, coffee would be good.'

'All right. Make yourself comfortable. I won't be a minute.'

'It's okay, I'll come outside with you.'

As they moved through to the kitchen, Laura wondered about the purpose of her next-door neighbour's visit. Laura had known the Kingsleys vaguely for two years, but the relationship had never progressed beyond a greetings card and a glass of sherry at Christmas. Clive was a retired bank manager who spent every spare moment off painting landscapes, while Mary was forever spending weeks at a time visiting friends down in London.

She turned to Karen and told her to take a seat at the breakfast bar. The teenager had a pleasant, round face and big, dark eyes. She was just over five feet in height and her red soft cotton two-piece spoke of calculated elegance. Beside her, Laura felt positively dowdy.

'How are you feeling now?' Karen asked. 'I mean . . . now that it's all over?'

Laura spooned coffee into a pair of mugs. 'I suppose I'm still numb, really,' she said after a moment. 'It hasn't sunk in yet.'

'That's what I thought,' Karen replied. 'You were pretty close to your mother, weren't you?'

'Yes.' To change the subject, she forced some brightness into her voice and asked, 'How do you like your coffee — black, white, strong, weak, with or without sugar?'

'As it comes.'

She switched the kettle on and

turned to face her guest, resting one hip against the worktop. 'Now — what was all that you were saying just now about being here to help me out? You've got me intrigued.'

'Well, I wouldn't want you to take offence, Laura. I mean, I know we've never been what you might call particularly close, but the way I see it, better late than never, eh?'

Laura frowned. 'You've lost me,' she said.

Karen sat back on her stool and crossed her legs. 'Well, don't think this is just me trying to do my good deed for the week, but — have you got anything planned for this afternoon?'

The question took Laura by surprise. 'Well, no, not really. Why?'

Again Karen could not restrain her grin. 'Because I'm going to take you out and buy you lunch.'

At that moment the kettle began to boil, and as she turned to make the coffee, Laura asked '*Me?* Why?'

'Why not?'

'There has to be *some* reason, surely.'

At that, Karen decided it was best to come clean. 'All right — it's not just my naturally generous spirit that's prompted the invite. The truth is, I've spent the whole of my summer holidays moping around Shepham. I'm bored stiff, and it's obvious that you need cheering up, too. So I thought, I know, it's such a lovely day, I'll see if Laura wants to go into Colbury with me this afternoon. Besides which, Garwood's is having a sale.'

'Garwood's?'

'Yes, you know, the fashion shop.'

Laura nodded in sudden recollection. 'The *exclusive* fashion shop,' she said.

Karen nodded. 'What do you say? A slap-up meal — well, the best I can afford, anyway. A look at some stunning designs. An afternoon of my undivided — not to mention scintillating — company.'

'Well . . . '

'Oh, go on. It'll do you good.'

There seemed to be something so

eager in the young girl's tone that Laura was prompted to say, 'I don't mean to sound ungrateful. I really *do* appreciate the offer. But why *me*, Karen? I'm sure you must have dozens of friends more your own age who you'd prefer to go with.'

Karen took a sip of coffee before replying. 'I have,' she said easily. 'But Colbury is about fifteen miles away, and you're the only person I know who's got a car.'

The answer was so blunt that Laura stared at her for a long moment, truly amazed. Then Karen suddenly burst into a fit of laughter, and despite everything, Laura found it difficult not to join in.

'Why else did you think I'd shell out to buy you lunch?' the teenager asked when they recovered. 'I mean, to have offered you petrol money would have been so *vulgar*.'

That sent them into another fit of hysterics.

Eventually Laura wiped at her eyes

and said on impulse, 'All right, you're on. You buy me lunch, and I'll run us into Colbury.'

Karen slipped down off her stool. 'Great! Look, I've got to dash. Thanks for the coffee. See you about one o'clock?'

Laura nodded. 'One o'clock it is,' she replied with a smile.

★   ★   ★

Derek Barber hardly ever called in to the office, even though it was only a short walk from his home. In fact, he hardly ever stirred from the cluttered study where he spent most of his days brooding.

Today, however, was different.

Having woken early and breakfasted on a lightly boiled egg and a single slice of dry toast while Shirley was still in bed, Derek had reached a decision. It was time to act. Of that he was sure. So, by the time Shirley was up and about, he was just straightening his dark blue tie and slipping into a grey sports' jacket.

Shirley, still clad in a dressing gown, watched as he checked his pockets. 'You're looking rather smart today, dear. Going anywhere special?'

Derek's bloodshot eyes grazed his wife briefly. He read concern in her expression, concern she had cleverly concealed from her tone, and suddenly felt an uncharacteristic surge of love for her.

Shirley. She had stuck by him through thick and thin. The ideal wife, he thought, a good ambassador, a charming conversationalist. More than one big deal had been clinched by the influence — he was almost tempted to call it *magic* — she had been able to exert over potential clients, back in the old days.

'I thought I'd pop in on Mark, see how things are going,' he said.

'Are you sure you're up to it?'

'I'm not an invalid.'

'Yes, I know. But I'm still worried by

that nasty turn you had at the funeral.'

'Don't fuss, woman. I feel fine today. Anyway, you're always on at me to get more exercise.'

'Well, give Mark my love,' she said.

Derek snorted. 'Are you sure you don't want me to blow his nose for him while I'm at it?'

Shortly afterward he left the house, crunching ponderously up the gravel drive, too wrapped up in his own thoughts to pause and wave to the wife who watched him worriedly from the front door.

This early in the day the office was empty of clients, and secretly it pleased him to be recognised so swiftly and greeted so warmly, particularly by the attractive young receptionist, Sarah Clarke.

Tall, lithe, with slim, pearl-grey glasses and her hair a mass of controlled copper curls, she exuded sophistication and confidence. She was going places, this one, only twenty-three years of age but destined for better things. Shepham wouldn't hold her for long, not like —

'Mr Barber, good morning!' She had left her desk to meet him, extending her cool right hand. 'We don't often get the pleasure of your company. Can I get you a cup of coffee?'

'Thanks. Actually, I'm here to see Mark. Is he in yet?'

'Out with a client. Please, take a seat. I don't suppose he'll be much longer.'

Derek sat down, returning the nods he received from the office's other occupants, a good, steady worker named Bill Everett and a newcomer he hadn't seen before. Then he returned his attention to Sarah, who was pouring him a cup of coffee from the pot on the hotplate.

'Important client, is it?' he asked when she came back.

'Who, with Mark, you mean?' she replied as she took her seat again. 'Fairly. Are you familiar with that old property just off the Cameron Road?'

'Used to be a vicarage?'

'That's the one — seven beds, three bathrooms, three receptions. Well, it's been on our books for about five months now. It's in need of major renovation, you see, and most of the potential buyers who've seen it just haven't been prepared to spend that kind of time and money on it.'

'But now you think you might have someone who is?'

'Exactly. A do-it-yourself fanatic, someone big in the city. I feel very optimistic.'

'Good, good.'

'Anyway, how are you keeping, Mr Barber? You're looking very well, I must say.'

'Oh, so-so. You know how it is.'

'I don't suppose the funeral was very easy for you. You must have known Mrs Jennings for a long time.'

'Thirty-five years,' he said.

'I know Mark was upset. He was very concerned for Mrs Jennings' daughter.'

Derek's expression hardened at the mention of Laura, but he refrained from offering any comment. 'How are things here apart from the Cameron Road property?' he asked.

She shrugged and sat back, looking every inch a top executive across the littered desk. Derek could hardly disguise his appreciation of her now. If Mark had to set his sights on a woman, why not this one?

'Well, there's the Mackenzie deal, of course.'

Derek nodded, his eyes suddenly animate. Ah yes, the Mackenzie deal, very nearly the biggest feather in Barber & Jennings' cap — 90,000 acres to the west of Shepham, close to the motor-way and less than an hour from London. A prime site currently being developed by Mackenzie Holdings.

In time, the businessman Neil Mack-enzie was going to build a whole new town there: houses, churches, a shop-ping mall, theatre and cinema. The new town — well, more an extension of Shepham itself, really — would have everything. It was an ambitious project that would take years to complete, but already interest was coming from industrial, commercial and residential quarters.

Mark had successfully negotiated the sale of the land earlier in the year, had helped Mackenzie's advisors to clear planning permission and ensure that a balanced view of the project was presented to the locals, who would otherwise have panicked at such a large-scale invasion. But now came his biggest challenge — to convince Mackenzie that Barber & Jennings should have sole representation of all the property he was going to build on the new site.

Derek wasn't sure his son could pull it off, not distracted as he was at the moment. Again he heard Sarah's words in his mind; *He was very concerned for Mrs Jennings' daughter.*

But Derek was damned if he would allow such a tremendous opportunity to slip through Mark's fingers all because of a silly slip of a girl like Laura Jennings —

'Mr Barber — are you all right?'

Derek blinked, saw Sarah studying him with concern, and forced his hands to unclench. 'Yes, fine. I — '

'Are you sure? You've gone as white as — '

Before she could say more, Sarah's attention was taken by something happening behind him. Derek turned just as Mark came through the door, looking very smart in a lightweight grey suit, ice-blue shirt and grey tie. His surprise at finding his father there was obvious.

'Dad! What is it? Is something wrong?'

'Just thought I'd drop by,' Derek said, rising to his feet. 'Have a chat, find out what's new. You know.'

'Coffee, Mark?' Sarah enquired as he started towards his own office at the back of the building.

'Please.'

Mark led the way and Derek followed. The office was small but tastefully decorated and scrupulously tidy. A moment later, while they were getting themselves settled, Sarah came in and put a cup down on Mark's desk. Derek watched her leave and close the door behind her. He had seen something in the way she had looked at Mark, something Mark had obviously missed, and immediately started plotting.

'You should watch that one, Mark,' he advised. 'With the right handling, she could become your best salesperson.'

Mark sampled his coffee. 'Oh, no doubt. Given time, she — '

'What do you mean, given time? The girl's a natural at this game.'

'I know,' Mark agreed again. 'But there's something about her . . . ' He paused, shook his head. 'She's not *immature*, exactly. Just the opposite, actually. Older than her years.'

'What are you going on about?'

'I just think she's a bit too confident for her own good,' Mark decided.

Derek frowned. 'Of course she's

confident! She's a saleswoman for God's sake! She *has* to be confident!'

Mark's face creased in a faint smile. 'I know that,' he repeated patiently. 'But times change, Dad. Prospective clients don't want the high-pressure sales techniques of yesterday any more. They're too sophisticated for that now. They want their estate agents to be people they feel they can really trust. I'm sorry, but that's just the way it is today.'

'And you don't think Sarah's got what it takes, eh?'

'I didn't say that. But I've seen her in action, and as soon as she starts the old hard-sell, she scares the clients off. The sooner she learns a little restraint the better.'

Derek made a dismissive sound in his throat, closing that particular line of conversation by means of a critical glance around the office.

'So — to what do we owe the pleasure of this little visit?' Mark asked politely.

'Oh, just thought I'd get out for an hour or so. Wanted to have a word with you about a few things. How did you get on with the Cameron Road property by the way?'

'Difficult to say. The client certainly *seemed* interested, but how often have we heard that one before?'

Derek shrugged. 'If you'd tried the old 'hard-sell', as you call it, you'd have shifted that place months ago,' he replied. 'Anyway, let's not argue about it. The main reason I called was to invite you over for dinner.'

Ignoring Mark's raised eyebrows, he went on, 'It's been a long time, and you know what your mother's like, she worries that you're not eating properly in that pokey little flat of yours.'

'Well . . . '

'Tonight? It'd give us the chance to discuss some of the finer points of the Mackenzie deal.'

Mark didn't reply straightaway, but whilst he appreciated the sudden resurgence of interest Derek seemed to be taking in the business, he didn't want his father looking over his shoulder every time he negotiated a big deal.

Still, it *had* been a long time since he'd visited his parents, and his mother was right, as always — he wasn't eating proper meals as often as he should.

'All right,' he said at last. 'What time?'

'About half past seven.' Derek climbed to his feet. 'Tell you what — bring young Sarah with you.'

'*What?*'

'She'll make up the numbers,' Derek went on. 'And I'll get the chance to see if she really is as over-confident as you say she is.'

Mark was now finding it very difficult to hide his irritation. 'Dad, I'm sure Sarah's got better things to do with her time than to — '

'Nonsense! She's a climber, that one. Think she'd refuse a dinner invitation from the man who put the Barber into Barber and Jennings?' Before Mark could protest further, Derek opened the office door and called out, 'Sarah — could you come here a moment, please?'

Mark sighed. He had the feeling he'd just been set up for something that was going to turn out highly unpleasant.

★ ★ ★

Laura was in much better spirits when she closed the front door behind Karen Kingsley, positively buoyant in comparison to the misery of the last couple of weeks. Then, turning back into the hallway, she caught another glimpse of herself in the full-length mirror, and studied her appearance more critically.

The pale yellow blouse was old, casual and familiar, the blue jeans and trainers comfortable but not exactly the height of fashion. After seeing the sophisticated elegance of a girl seven years her junior, Laura suddenly felt herself coming back down to earth. Yet again she realised that it was going to be hard work to make up for all those lost years.

But at least she could try.

With that thought in mind, she went into her bedroom and opened the doors to her wardrobe. There were some dresses, a few pairs of casual and fairly smart trousers, blouses, tee-shirts, a couple of neat jackets, but nothing that could really compete with the style that Karen had shown this morning.

Still, she wasn't going into Colbury with the younger girl in order to *compete* with her. Rummaging through the wardrobe, she at last came across a neat orange and lemon tropical print dress. This, together with a smart pair of low-heeled, button-strap court shoes, would certainly spice up her otherwise dated image.

Satisfied, Laura now peered into the dressing-table mirror, paying special attention to her face. Her skin was clear and fresh from years of clean country air, her hazel eyes large, sparking orbs, her nose slightly snubbed and her lips full, but she had to admit that the kindest thing she could say about herself was that she was presentable, if nothing more.

But again she was being over-critical, for when she studied herself closer in the mirror's reflection, she realised that by experimenting a little with make-up, she could actually accentuate the fine, strong features she had inherited from her parents.

In any case, she had nothing to lose by trying.

She glanced at her wristwatch. It was 10:45 now. She had just over two hours before she and Karen set off for Colbury. Looking at the reflection staring back at her, she decided that she would put that time to good use — clear up the things still scattered everywhere in her mother's room, then shower, shampoo her hair and begin the transformation from presentable into something much more.

3

Karen Kingsley turned up promptly at one o'clock, and within minutes the two girls had driven off in Laura's red VW Polo.

Colbury turned out to be a veritable maze of a town that dated back to the fifteenth century, full of narrow, cobbled streets housing numerous olde-worlde shops as well as a larger, more up-to-date shopping complex. When at last they found a parking space, however, it was a very different Laura who emerged from the car.

It was in her face that the change was most evident, for a mixture of eye-shadow, applied in subtle sweeps, had brought out the appealing, child-like roundness of her eyes, just as a little mascara had made the most of her long lashes. A gentle application of blusher added to the natural glow of her cheeks, and her full lips now shimmered with a hint of cinnamon.

At one o'clock, Karen had not been able to hide her surprise upon seeing Laura for the first time after the transformation, and though she had refrained from comment, Laura had found the girl's reaction gratifying.

Now the two new friends window-shopped the length of picturesque Moorstan Row, then made their way down into the centre of town, where, true to her word, Karen bought them lunch in a pleasant little Italian restaurant called Lettieri's.

After lunch, they wandered around Colbury's flea-market, then on to Garwood's, the exclusive fashion shop in which Karen had shown so much interest earlier.

Here they browsed the shop's four spot-lit floors, studying the spectacular fashions of the brightest young designers. Eventually, and after much internal debate, Karen threw caution to the wind and bought a black and white jacket and slim-line pleated silk skirt that was outrageous in both style and price.

Once they were out in the sunshine again, it was back along Potter Lane to an old-fashioned tea room, where they took an umbrella-shaded table on the paved forecourt. Karen insisted on ordering iced tea and cream cakes — and Laura insisted on paying for them.

As they waited for their order to come, Laura glanced at the happy, animated faces of the people around her. The late afternoon sun was still pleasantly warm, and the babble of chatter around them was comforting. It felt good to be here, away from the memories waiting for her back in Shepham.

'What are you thinking about?' Karen asked suddenly.

Laura turned her attention back to her new friend and indicated the large plastic bag beside Karen's seat, which contained the young girl's reckless purchases. '*That*,' she replied. 'I was just wondering how you could possibly afford it.'

'I can't,' Karen grinned in reply. 'But my dad used to be a bank manager, don't forget. He told me all about overdrafts and what they're for.'

After the waitress brought their iced tea and cakes, Laura asked, 'When do you go back to college?'

Karen helped herself to a doughnut. 'About two weeks' time.'

'What are you studying?'

'Graphic design.' Karen chewed steadily, and with such relish that Laura was prompted to help herself from the fattening pile. 'That's my dad coming out in me again, you see. Artistic.' She sipped at her iced tea. 'How about you? Ever though about a career, or further education or anything?'

'Not really. Not until now.'

'What would you like to do?'

'I really haven't given it much thought. The truth is — '

She paused.

43

'Go on.'

'Well, I suppose the truth is that up until now I've never really *needed* to plan my life. Each day was exactly like the one before. Until my mother died, there was never any need to wonder what lay ahead, or attempt to steer things in a particular direction.'

'Well, what are you interested in?' Karen pursued.

'Travel, writing. All sorts of things, really.'

'Then why don't you have a go at being a travel writer?'

'Well, I don't suppose it's as easy as that.'

'Maybe not. But it's worth a try, surely?'

'I might, then.'

'That means you won't.'

Laura's good mood slipped a little. 'To be honest,' she confessed, 'I really don't know *what* to do with myself.'

Karen offered her an understanding smile. 'Well, make your mind up soon, Laura. You've got to grab every opportunity while you can. If you don't, you'll wake up one day with a husband and fifty screaming children, and then it'll be too late to do *anything*.'

Laura smiled briefly. 'A husband and fifty screaming children?' she repeated.

'Well, maybe forty-nine children. But you know what I mean. Not that I've got anything against marriage and procreation.'

'It's just that they're not for you,' Laura prompted, turning the conversation around so that she was the questioner.

'Not yet, at any rate. Once I've *done* something with my life, *become* someone, then I'll think about marriage and a family. You're all for it, I assume?'

Laura glanced up at the people coming and going around them. 'I always wanted a career, a husband, a family, yes. But somewhere along the line, I suppose I just resigned myself to leading a very different sort of existence.'

'So there isn't anyone in your life at the moment?'

The very idea seemed laughable. 'Good grief, no,' she replied.

'Not even that tall guy I've seen popping in and out all the time?'

'Tall guy?'

'The one with the smart suits and the sandy hair. Quite good-looking. About your age.'

'Oh, you mean Mark. No, Mark and I, we're more like brother and sister than anything else.'

'Still, he's very good-looking.'

'Yes, I suppose he is.'

A half-hour sit in the sinking sun was very pleasant, and afterwards, the two girls wandered back through the flea-market and decided on impulse to visit Colbury's biggest department store while they were there. It was as they were passing through the stationery department that Laura suddenly had an idea. Telling Karen of her intention, they made their way over to a display of pens and pencils.

'Mark's always going on about not having a decent pen to impress his clients with,' she explained as they studied the display. 'I was going to get him one last Christmas, but then my mother took a turn for the worse and somehow I never got around to it.'

After some deliberation, Laura selected a smart-looking fountain pen, matt black with a gold-plated trim, and the purchase cheered her up considerably. She could hardly wait to see Mark's face when she presented it to him.

★　★　★

They got back at about five o'clock, and Laura dropped Karen outside her parents' cottage before parking the Polo in her own drive.

She stepped out of the car, left her bag on the seat but took out the package she'd had gift-wrapped in the department store. With a faint smile lighting her face, she started off on the fondly-remembered trek up to High Road.

The estate agency office stayed open

late on summer evenings, and sure enough, the atmosphere was still brisk when she stepped inside a little after five. Bill Everett was discussing business with a young married couple, and an employee she hadn't seen before was on the phone to someone and glancing at his watch. Sarah Clarke, the receptionist, looked up as she came in, and stood up to greet her.

Her appraisal of Laura more of a professional sizing-up than anything else, and her blue eyes, behind her narrow pearly-grey glasses, lingered speculatively on the package she held in her hands.

'It's Laura Jennings, isn't it?' she said.

Laura smiled, but before she could reply, Sarah extended her right hand and went on, 'I'm Sarah Clarke. How do you do? I was very sorry to hear about your mother.'

'Thank you.' Glancing over Sarah's shoulder, she asked, 'Is Mark in?'

'Yes. Just wait a moment and I'll go

48

and tell him you're here.'

Left alone, Laura glanced around the office. How it had changed since the days when she used to come up to meet her father on sunny summer's evenings just like this. The newcomer on the phone glanced up and, catching her eye, smiled. Laura nodded a greeting.

'Hello, Laura!'

She turned just as Sarah swept past her to resume her seat and Mark appeared from his private office, looking very casual with his shirtsleeves rolled up and his tie loosened.

But as she turned to face him he suddenly froze, and whatever he'd been about to say died on his tongue.

The transformation was so unexpected that Laura actually opened her mouth to ask him what was wrong. But then, in that instant before she spoke, realisation struck her.

The dress, the shoes, the make-up — it was the first time he had seen her in her new guise.

At once she felt a blush burning her

cheeks, and glanced down at her feet. She'd had an entire afternoon to lose her self-consciousness, but now it came flooding back to engulf her. Sarah, watching the moment closely but not understanding it, frowned.

Then life — which had been suspended for no more than two or three seconds — started up again.

Mark recovered first. 'I . . . Come on through.' As he ushered her into his office, he went on, 'I called you a couple of times this afternoon. You know, just to see how you were.'

'I went into Colbury with the girl next door.'

'Oh, I know the one. I met her father once or twice, before he retired.' He moved around his desk. 'Take a seat.'

While he appeared to have recovered from his momentary surprise, Laura's tummy was still fluttering with the realisation of what she thought she had seen in his eyes.

'Well,' he said awkwardly. 'This makes a pleasant change. I can't remember the last time you popped in.'

She glanced down at the brightly-wrapped package balanced in her lap. Suddenly she wasn't so sure that the gift was a good idea. But it was too late now: the wrapping was so colourful that he could hardly have failed to notice it.

'How are things, anyway? I've been meaning to drop by, but we've been so busy here, what with this blasted Mackenzie business and everything.'

Laura frowned, anxious to steer the conversation onto safer ground. 'What's the Mackenzie business?'

'Oh, nothing. It's not important.'

'It must be. Go on, tell me, if you like.'

At her urging, he explained all about Neil Mackenzie and his plans for New Shepham, as he was hoping to call it, adding that his father was already finding it hard not to interfere in negotiations.

'I'm glad he's taking an interest,' Mark said. 'But he's still living in the past. A lot of things have changed in the last couple of years. If Dad had his way, he'd just wade in and blow the whole deal.'

Laura nodded, finding it easy to understand how Derek could put his son in this awkward position. 'Who is this Mackenzie, anyway?' she asked.

'Oh, the City's latest whiz-kid,' he replied wearily. 'He inherited Mackenzie Holdings from his father three years ago, when he was about the age we are now. Everyone said that it was commercial suicide to hand such a huge conglomerate over to someone who'd never shown the remotest interest in business before, but apparently his father doted on him and wouldn't be swayed from his decision.'

'What happened?' Laura asked, feeling herself beginning to relax at last.

'The old man died, Neil took over,' Mark replied. 'And Mackenzie Holdings' profits rose by thirty percent within his first financial year as company chairman. He bought two more companies to add to an already burgeoning list and created another, something to do with compact disc manufacture, which seems to be going from strength to strength. His board of directors are happy, the shareholders are happy. Everybody's happy.'

By contrast, Mark did not sound at all happy.

'And his latest project,' Laura murmured, 'is New Shepham.'

'Exactly,' he said.

She narrowed her hazel eyes. 'Why don't you like him?'

Her question was so blunt that he appeared startled for a moment before smiling mirthlessly. 'Because he's arrogant,' he replied. 'He thinks all he has to do is snap his fingers and everyone around him will jump to do his bidding. He's that kind of man, full of his own importance. You know, just once . . . '

'What?'

'Just once I'd like someone to say 'no' to him for a change.'

Silence descended on the small office until Mark's mood brightened a little.

'Anyway, enough shop-talk. How are you?'

'Fine.'

'*Really?*'

'Really.'

'You look well, I must say,' he admitted. 'In fact, I've never seen you look *quite* so well.'

Her eyes fell to the square package in her hands, and to shift his attention from her face she passed it across to him so abruptly that he had no option but to accept it.

'What's this?' he asked.

'Open it and find out,' she replied.

He set the package down, then smiled and proceeded to tear away the bright wrapping. Soon he was holding a plain white box in his firm, long-fingered hands.

'What *is* this?' he said again, more than a little embarrassed. 'Did I forget my own birthday or something?'

Laura said, 'I'll tell you what I told Karen Kingsley this afternoon. I wouldn't have gotten through this if it hadn't been for you. *That*,' she indicated the package, 'is just my way of saying thanks.'

He stared at her for a moment, then opened the box.

His laugh released some of the awkwardness building in the little office as he took out a miniature galvanised dustbin about eight inches high.

'I know what you're like for being neat and tidy,' Laura explained, feeling better about the gift now that she had seen his reaction. 'You can keep it on your desk and put all your odds and ends in it.'

His smile was broad and boyish, but just as he was about to thank her, he heard something rattle inside the bin. Once again his frown asked the question.

'One more,' she said softly.

He took the lid off the bin and took out the long, slim package within. Carefully he took off the wrapping and opened the presentation case.

Catching the light, the gold-plated fountain pen winked up at him richly.

'Use it to impress Neil Mackenzie,' she said.

He took the pen out and examined it more closely. 'I never expected anything like this . . . ' he began.

'You never expect *anything*,' she reminded him.

Then he broke into another smile. 'Thank you. Thank you very much indeed.'

Laura got to her feet. 'Well, I'd better be on my way,' she said. 'What with one thing and another, it's been a long day.'

He stood with her and came around the desk, still holding the pen. 'Thanks again for this, Laura. I really *do* appreciate it, you know.'

He leaned forward and kissed her affectionately on the cheek, and they were so close in that moment that she could smell his aftershave and feel a hint of five o'clock shadow brushing gently at her face, and all at once her heart hammered and the breath caught in her throat.

She fought the urge to panic and pull

away. It was just a brotherly peck, that was all. But never before had she been so aware of him as a *man*, and that was the scary part.

When she heard the brisk rap at the door she jumped and took a step away from him just as Sarah Clarke popped her copper-curled head into the room and looked curiously from one of them to the other.

'I'm off now,' she said, her expression changing subtly when her eyes settled on Mark. 'But I'll see you later. What time did you say you'd be picking me up?'

Marked looked as uncomfortable as Laura had felt. 'About seven-fifteen,' he replied.

Sarah's smile was bright and satisfied. 'See you later, then. Goodbye, Miss Jennings.'

Then she was gone, leaving the two lifelong friends to say uncomfortable farewells of their own.

★ ★ ★

Despite having been informed about Derek's dinner invitation at the last moment, Shirley Barber managed to concoct a meal that was both memorable and delicious by the time Mark and Sarah turned up at seven-thirty that evening.

Over pre-dinner drinks on the patio, where a pleasant breeze relieved some of the day's lingering heat, Derek, no doubt determined to prove his son's judgement wrong, began a none-too-subtle interrogation of the redhead, only to find that they agreed on virtually everything.

Mark wisely kept out of the conversation and contented himself with an occasional sip of wine as he stared moodily off into the leafy distance. In some strange, indefinable way, it annoyed him that Sarah and his father should get on so well, but after a while he realised that it was simply because the two of them were birds of a feather: that the very traits he hoped Sarah would lose or tone down in order to improve herself both personally and professionally, were the same qualities that he found so disturbing in his father.

But tonight there was something else eating at him, something he didn't really want to think about but could not *help* thinking about.

Laura.

He took another sip of wine. The chatter and laughter from across the room washed over him unheeded.

At last Sarah excused herself for a moment, and Derek came across to him, for once his yellowish face positively beaming.

'You want to watch that one,' he said, repeating the same phrase he'd used in connection with Sarah earlier. 'Over-confident? Never heard anything so daft! Hang on to her Mark, that's my advice. She's got everything — wit, style, determination. Encourage her. Give her more responsibility. Involve her in the Mackenzie deal if you like — I'm sure Neil Mackenzie has an eye for a pretty girl.'

Mark remained preoccupied right through the meal, although he managed to say all the right things at all the right moments. After the last bowl had been cleared away, all four retired to the lounge, and while Sarah began to skilfully insinuate herself into Shirley's affections, Derek began to lay out various strategies for Mark to employ with his dealings with the chairman of Mackenzie Holdings — all of which Sarah heartily endorsed.

'Your parents are lovely people,' she told him later, as he drove her home through Shepham's dark, sleeping streets. Her voice was deep, husky, slightly slurred.

He kept his eyes on the road ahead.

'Your father's lost none of his edge,' she went on admiringly. 'Fascinating man. Very forceful. I wonder . . . '

'Wonder what?' he asked when she fell silent.

'Well . . . I know it's not really my place to say, but . . . your father knows more about our business than anyone I've ever met. It just occurred to me what a dreadful waste it is for someone like that to have taken early retirement.'

Mark didn't comment.

'Why don't you ask him to come back to work?' she said.

He did glance at her then. '*What?*'

'Oh, only part time, of course. Perhaps in an advisory cap . . . capacity.'

She was drunk, or at least well on the way to being so. She must have been to make a suggestion like that, he thought wryly. He turned a corner, followed the narrow road half-way down to a block of recently-constructed flats and then pulled in, turning in his seat to face her.

The street was dark, and the light from the lamppost ten yards further along cast a weak, intimate glow across her face, reflecting from the dark pools of her glasses.

'Will you be all right?' he asked.

She nodded, and giggled a little. 'Yes.' She released the seatbelt: it slid back across her neat cream blouse like a snake. 'Thank you for a very en . . .

61

enjoyable evening.'

Then she leaned forward and planted a kiss firmly on his lips.

In the confines of the car he was trapped, held captive by his own seatbelt and thus unable to pull away. But in any case, the kiss was loose, all one-sided: he found the mixture of scent and alcohol nauseating.

At last, as if sensing his distaste, she sat back and gave him a long, searching look.

'You *do* know what I'm offering you?' she said quietly.

He returned her gaze levelly. 'Go to bed,' he told her. 'And go to sleep. I'll see you at work in the morning.'

She frowned at him, obviously unused to rejection. 'What is it? Is there someone else?'

The slur of her words told him all he needed to know. There was no real harm done — she would remember little if any of this tomorrow. 'Good night, Sarah,' he said firmly but not unkindly.

She sat there a moment longer, looking at him, then got out of the car and made her uncertain way up the flagstone path towards the entrance of the flats. He watched her fumble for a key in her bag, let herself inside, saw her figure through the frosted glass as she waited for the lift.

He shook his head. She'd asked him if there was someone else. Before today he would have said no. But now he knew that there *was* someone else, that there had *always* been someone else.

The only trouble was, to that someone else he would never be more than a big, adopted brother.

4

Over the next week or so, Laura continued to apply for jobs, but whenever she had to give details of her qualifications and previous work history, there was little to say, and inevitably that went against her.

Physically, however, she began to change almost beyond recognition. Influenced by Karen Kingsley, who became a constant companion in the days following that afternoon trek into Colbury, she began to dress with more thought than ever before, and experiment with make-up in order to find the subtle shades of colour that were just right for her.

Inside, though, she remained the same naïve and inexperienced child/woman she had always been, and in some ways that was how she wanted to stay, for the memory of how Mark had looked at her that afternoon in his office continued to haunt her. In those few fleeting seconds all barriers between them had disappeared. They were no longer 'family', but purely and simply a man and a woman, and the realisation of that both excited and terrified her.

Still, she could not allow memories — real or imagined — to rule her life. In any case, it had seemed from their brief conversation that day that there was something between Mark and Sarah that she, Laura, had no right to intrude upon.

About a week later, she was working out in the garden when the living room phone rang. With a frown she rose to her feet, pulled off her gloves and hurried inside.

'Hello?'

For a moment there was no answer. Then a familiar voice said, 'Hello, it's me.'

Laura's attractive face creased in a smile. 'Who's *me*?' she asked impishly.

At the other end of the line Karen

laughed. 'Don't be silly. Just how many *me*'s do you know?'

'Oh, only a few thousand.'

'Well this is *me* me. I didn't disturb you from anything, did I? I was just about to hang up when you answered.'

'I was out in the garden.'

'Oh. Well, sorry if I dragged you away from anything desperate, but I'm staying at Gillian's at the moment, that's why I'm phoning and not just poking my head over the garden wall.'

'Gillian?'

'Yes, you know, Gill Lewis, one of my friends from college. I'm always talking about her. Well, she's having a party at her place on Saturday night, you know, one mad fling before we all go back to boring old study, and I thought it would be great if you came along too — '

'Whoa,' Laura interrupted again. 'Before you get *too* carried away, let me have my say. It's very sweet of you to think of me, Karen, and I do appreciate the invitation — '

'That means you're going to say no.'

'What I'm going to say is that they're *your* friends, and probably *years* younger than me. I'd feel out of place.'

'You'd be surprised,' said Karen. 'Some of them are positively *ancient*.'

'You know what I mean.'

'I suppose so. But I really wish you'd come, Laura. Everyone'll be there.'

'Exactly. Everyone I don't know.'

Karen paused for a second. 'Look, hang on a minute, will you?'

'But — '

There was some noise in the background, and then a new voice came on the line, soft and pleasant. 'Hello, is that Laura?'

'Yes.'

'Hi, I'm Gill. Listen, you simply *must* come to my party, I insist. Don't worry about who you know and who you don't. Little things like that don't matter at do's like this.'

'Well — '

'Oh, you *must*. I'll never get any peace from Karen if you don't. You know how childish she can be when she puts her mind to it.'

Laura's hazel eyes were on the bright, clean sunshine spilling across the lawn, spot-lighting colourful bursts of fuschia, geranium and godetia. The sky was pure blue and the scent of summer was heavy in her nostrils. She felt good, better than she had for months, and pleased to be wanted. Maybe she shouldn't dismiss such a kind invitation out of hand.

Taking a deep breath, she told the other girl, 'Well, I wouldn't want to spoil your friendship with Karen just by saying no. If you're sure that — '

'Oh brill!' Much to her relief, Gill sounded genuinely pleased by her acceptance. 'I'm really glad, Laura. It'll be great to meet you, I'm sure.'

In the background, Karen gave an ear-splitting cheer.

'I'm sure it will be mutual.'

Suddenly she was glad she'd said yes.

★ ★ ★

68

'Mark?'

Mark looked up from the documents scattered across his desk. In the soft glow of the desk lamp he looked tired and overworked. Even the ticking of the wall clock, signalling the end of another hectic day, seemed to come only with effort.

Standing in his office doorway, Sarah Clarke stared down at him with concern. 'I'm off now,' she said.

He nodded and cleared his throat. 'Okay, Sarah. See you in the morning.'

'Yes.'

But she continued to stand there. 'Mark — is there anything troubling you?'

He frowned.

'You've been very quiet ever since we went to your parents for dinner.'

'I've just been extra busy, I suppose.'

Her expression was doubtful. 'Are you sure you're not sickening for something?'

'Sure.' He forced a smile onto his weary countenance. 'But thank you for asking.'

She nodded, then slowly backed away. 'Goodnight, then.'

'Goodnight, Sarah.'

He heaved a sigh of relief when he heard the door close behind her.

He had tried hard to keep a low profile in the week following her drunken pass at him, but apparently Sarah had no memory of the incident. The very next morning she had arrived for work pale and subdued, but he'd put that down to the after-effects of all the wine she'd consumed. After that, office life soon settled back into its familiar busy pattern.

But now Mark could not shake his uncomfortable awareness of the way she looked at him, listened to him, deliberately engaged him in conversation and always went all-out to impress him. Suddenly his imagination found all manner of hidden meanings in even her most innocent comments.

Or *was* it his imagination?

He wasn't so sure.

It was ridiculous, of course, but

suddenly he felt threatened by her presence. She was, he felt, a predator . . . and if she had anything to do with it, he was about to become her prey.

★   ★   ★

As Saturday approached, Laura began to doubt the wisdom of having accepted the party invitation. She had always been shy and retiring. Now she would be walking into a room full of people — worse, complete *strangers*. She would feel out of place, a dusty old relic among so many bright young things. And what on earth would she find to talk about? Her fellow guests were students, people of high education, and her own schooling had ended at the age of sixteen. They would find her old, dull and boring —

It was fortunate that Karen was always on hand to curb her rising panic. Really, without her Laura would never have found the courage to go through with it.

But when Saturday finally arrived, go through with it she did.

Gill Lewis lived with her parents in an attractive town house about six miles away in neighbouring Knightly, but since they were away, Gill had decided to throw a party for all her friends before their reluctant return to college.

The party was already in full swing when Laura and Karen arrived at seven-thirty. As they stepped out of Laura's car into the pleasant late summer's evening, the pounding of loud music could be heard right across the street.

The butterflies dancing in Laura's tummy must have made themselves obvious by the expression on her face, because Karen chuckled and said, 'Come on, you're here to enjoy yourself, remember?'

Laura smiled and together they made their way up the neat front path. Karen was wearing the black and white jacket and pleated silk skirt she'd bought that afternoon in Colbury. Beside her, Laura looked smart in a figure-clinging emerald green dress over which she wore a crisp white shirt fastened at the waist by a matching green cummerbund.

A young man in his early twenties with a mouthful of canapé opened the door and waved them in. In the through-lounge food and drink had been arranged on two long tables, but to get to it they had to find a route between twenty or thirty couples dancing energetically to the throb of heavy rock music.

Karen seemed to slip into the party spirit almost at once, but Laura knew immediately that all her worst fears had come true. She was out of place here. She turned to tell Karen as much but the words died in her throat when she realised that Karen was no longer beside her. Peering hastily around the darkened room, she caught sight of her young friend dancing with a smiling boy several couples away.

'You must be Laura.'

She turned abruptly to find herself face to face with a girl about her own age or maybe slightly younger, with long fair hair spilling from a centre parting and a round face with brown eyes, a snubbed nose and a wide, smiling mouth.

'I'm Gill,' said the girl, shouting to make herself heard. She took Laura by one arm and guided her from what had become the dance floor. 'Karen never was very big on introductions, I'm afraid.'

As soon as they were on the sidelines, Gill asked Laura what she wanted to drink.

'Oh . . . pineapple juice, please.'

'Pineapple juice? You haven't signed the Pledge, I hope?'

Laura smiled. 'No, but I'm driving.'

'Oh, don't worry about that. If you get too zonked to drive you can always crash here. I don't mind.'

'Well, thanks. But I think I'd better stick to soft drinks all the same.'

Gill shrugged. 'If you're sure. Plenty

of booze here if you fancy it, though. I tell you, Laura, we're in for a wild time if I've got anything to do with it. Anything goes tonight!'

She thrust a paper cup of pineapple juice into Laura's hand so roughly that some of the liquid slopped over the rim and spilled across her dress.

'Oh — !'

But Gill was already moving off, shouting over her shoulder, ''Scuse me, love. Must mingle and all that!'

Laura stood there in the dark, smoky room feeling wretched. Once she caught sight of Karen dancing with another young man, and for a moment envied her friend the ability to simply relax, mix and enjoy herself.

She took a sip of the pineapple juice, then set the cup down on the table. Looking around, all she saw were couples and groups, no other single person with whom she could pass the time in casual conversation. She supposed that there must be seventy people jammed into the room, plus another twenty chatting out in the hallway or in the cool back garden.

The heavy rock music ended. For one brief moment she heard laughter, the buzz of conversation, the clink of glasses. Then another song began pounding at full volume. She sighed and reached for her drink, then froze.

Someone had used her cup as an ash-tray. A cigarette end floated in the remains of her pineapple juice.

The sigh that escaped her was lost beneath the bedlam of noise. She moved away from the table, hoping to put some distance between herself and the distorted racket belching from the CD system.

A young girl with a crew-cut of spiky white hair appeared in her path. Laura fixed a smile onto her otherwise strained face and said hello, but the girl pushed past and disappeared, having given no sign that she'd even heard the greeting.

She found an unoccupied nook and stood there, willing the time to pass quickly. Glancing to her left, she saw a couple engaged in some very heavy petting. To her right someone spilled a bowl of coleslaw onto the carpet and howled with laughter.

She glanced at her wristwatch. What had seemed to be hours was in fact barely twenty minutes.

She sighed again. Gill walked past. 'Having a good time, Lucy? You look like you are, I must say.' Then she was gone.

Lucy, Laura thought. *I'm so anonymous that people can't even remember my name now.*

Fifteen minutes later the constant throb of rock music and the thick, cloying scents of alcohol had given her an eye-blurring headache. Somehow she managed to make her way outside to the patio to get some fresh air. Nearby, about seven youths were trying to get a fire started in the barbecue pit.

Laura looked at her watch again. How could one hour seem like so many?

'Cheer up, love, it might never happen.'

Mark looked up into the smiling face of the *Goose and Gander*'s landlady, Ellen Dean, and asked, 'Do I really look that bad?'

'Let's just say I've seen happier-looking funeral directors,' she quipped.

He raised his empty glass. 'Well, we can't have that, can we? Bad for trade. Better refresh this, I think.'

Ellen took the glass and pulled another pint. 'Got anything special planned for tonight?' she asked.

'No.'

'No hot date?'

'Not even a lukewarm one, I'm sorry to say.'

'But it's Saturday night, Mark! A smart young man like you — '

Before she could pursue the subject, another customer caught her eye and she hurried off to serve him, leaving Mark alone with his thoughts. And like it or not, he had plenty to think *about*.

She was right, of course. But though he'd had a string of girlfriends in the past, none of them had lasted, and he'd always blamed himself, figuring that he just wasn't interesting enough for them.

Now, though, he realised that it was because they had always somehow sensed that his heart just wasn't in it, that his heart, in fact, was elsewhere.

They were right.

He had no idea when he had stopped seeing Laura as a sister-figure and fallen in love with her. She had always been there, and he had naturally assumed that she would *always* be there, good old Laura, everybody's friend.

But when he saw her on the day she had given him the pen, she had looked so . . . *different*. And that difference had finally made him understand that she was no longer a girl. She was a *woman* now, and that revelation also made him understand how he really felt about her.

The question now, though, was what

to *do* about it? Dare he actually try to *date* her? What if she said no, found the very idea distasteful because she had always seen him as more of a brother than anything else?

The last thing he wanted to do was spoil their relationship. Maybe it would be better to sound her out first, try to decide how *she* felt about things.

One thing was certain: he had to do *something* about the way he felt.

He decided to call her later this evening.

★ ★ ★

Laura lifted to tip-toe, hoping to find Karen, but couldn't see her anywhere. She couldn't even spy Gill mingling with the other guests.

'Lost someone?'

The speaker was a tall man with a shock of dark hair falling across his high forehead. He smiled and raised one eyebrow to emphasise his question.

'I'm sorry?' she said, lifting her voice.

80

'I said 'have you lost someone?' '

She shook her head because it was easier than having to shout. Catching her meaning, he threw a glance at the source of the din. 'Yes, it *is* a bit noisy in here, isn't it? Come on, let's go outside.'

Before she could protest, he took hold of her left hand and led her between the gyrating dancers and into the hallway, and from there out to the empty front garden, where they sat on the low stone wall beside the pavement.

'Well,' he said with a sigh, 'that's better.'

'Yes.'

He stuck out his right hand. 'I'm Keith, by the way. How do you do?'

She took his hand and they shook. 'Laura Jennings,' she said.

In the bright yellow glow of the streetlights, she saw that he was somewhere between twenty-five and thirty, with mysterious dark eyes, a small nose and a wide, smiling mouth. Beneath his neat open-necked white shirt and smart grey trousers he appeared to have a very athletic build. He looked husky, dependable, the friend of which she was at that moment so sorely in need.

'If you don't mind my saying so, Laura, you looked as if you badly needed rescuing from all that,' he said.

'Well, to be honest, I'm not much of a party-goer at the best of times, so this really isn't my cup of tea.'

He nodded. 'I know the feeling. So far I've hated every minute of it.'

'Then why did you come?'

'Why did *you*?'

She shrugged. 'I was invited by a friend.'

'So was I. Well, not so much invited as roped-in.'

'You're not a student then? I mean, you're not from the college?'

'Good Lord, no!' he chuckled. 'No, I'm in something far more routine. Accountancy. What about you? What do *you* do?'

She threw a glance up and down the

empty street. 'Nothing, yet.'

'Unemployed, eh?' he said sympathetically.

'Well, not quite.'

He indicated the house behind them, where the music was almost rattling the windows in their frames. 'They seem like a mad lot,' he commented.

'Yes.'

'What happened to your friend?' he asked suddenly. 'I assume he's the one you were looking for just now?'

'*She*,' Laura corrected, and almost at once regretted it, for suddenly he seemed to see her in a new light. No longer was she just someone he'd met at a party and chatted to for a few pleasant moments. Now she was an *unattached girl*.

But was that so bad? What was she afraid of, anyway? So far he had been very polite and very pleasant.

'I . . . ' she paused, swallowed, tried again. 'I don't know what happened to her. One moment she was there, the next she was off dancing.'

'Would *you* like to dance?' he asked, as if the idea had just occurred to him.

Laura touched fingertips to forehead. 'I don't think so. I'm afraid all that noise has given me a headache.'

'Actually, now that you mention it, you *do* look a bit pale.'

'Yes, I think I'd be better off going home.'

'You could be right. Would you like me to find your friend and tell her for you?'

'No, that's all right, I can manage. But thanks anyway.' She stood up and looked down at him. His face was a picture of understanding. 'It was very nice to talk to you,' she said.

'Me you too,' he replied. 'Take care of yourself, won't you?'

Reluctantly she went back into the house, where the air was hot, stuffy and grey with a vast accumulation of cigarette smoke.

Gill's round face suddenly appeared in front of her. 'All right, Lucy, love?'

Laura saw no point in correcting her.

'Fine thanks,' she lied. 'Have you seen Karen anywhere?'

The fair-haired girl shrugged. 'All over the place,' she replied carelessly. Laura recoiled from the wash of alcohol on her breath. 'For all I know she might even be up on the ceiling by now.'

'Thanks.'

She pushed through the throng blocking the hallway and quickly scanned the darkened dance floor. At last she spotted Karen over by the food table, piling a paper plate high with more chicken legs, sausage rolls and canapés than she could ever hope to eat. With more than a little difficulty, Laura crossed the room to stand beside her.

Karen looked around as she came up, her face showing surprise. She, too, looked somewhat the worse for drink. 'Hello, Laura. Where you been hiding?'

Laura had to shout to make herself heard, and that did nothing to improve the way she felt. 'Look, I've got a splitting headache and I'm going home, but will you be — '

'A splitting headache?' slurred Karen.

Laura nodded. 'Yes, but will you be all right here? I mean, were you relying on me for a lift home?'

'Lift — ? Oh no! I'm going to stay here and party the night away!'

'I'll sit out in the car until you're ready to go, if you like. I don't m — '

'Nah. Go, go.'

'Are you sure you'll be all right?'

Karen nodded emphatically. ''Course. Havin' a great time!'

And so saying, she turned away from Laura to continue filling her plate.

Laura struggled back across the room and out into the street. Much to her surprise, Keith was still standing by the front gate.

'Find her all right?' he asked gently.

'Yes, thanks.'

'Right.' He indicated the cars parked opposite with a nod of his dark head. 'Which one's yours?'

Mystified, she mumbled, 'The Polo.'

'All right,' he said. 'Give me the keys

and I'll go start her up.'

His suggestion was voiced so casually that for a split second it seemed the most natural thing in the world that he should do. But then warning bells jangled in Laura's already punished head.

'There's no need,' she said.

'Come on,' he urged, smiling. 'There's no way I'd just let you drive off with a blinding headache. I'd never forgive myself if anything happened to you.'

'But — '

'Come on,' he repeated, holding out his right hand. 'It's all right. I'm a friend. As soon as you're safely home I'll catch a bus back here, or something.'

Maybe he was right. She certainly didn't feel up to the drive home yet. She reached into her purse and drew out her keys.

'Where do you live?' he asked as he took them.

'Shepham.'

'Oh, I know it. Straight along the

Bathwood Road and then up to Alfort, right?'

'Yes.'

'Come on then, hop in,' he invited enthusiastically. 'I'll have you home in two ticks.'

5

Laura felt herself growing more anxious by the second as Keith propelled her car along darkened country lanes at an alarming rate.

Exactly what were his intentions? Was he really as considerate as he had first appeared, or had something else prompted his offer to drive her home?

She kept her eyes fixed firmly on the gravel road ahead. Perhaps she was panicking needlessly. But what did she really know about this man apart from his name and profession? And even then, what proof did she have that he was who he *said* he was?

Calm down, calm down . . .

'How are you feeling now?' he asked suddenly, breaking the oppressive silence.

She took her eyes off the road long enough to glance at his profile. He appeared to be genuinely concerned, but how could she be sure?

'Better,' she lied. 'Thank you.'

'Good.'

As he checked the rear-view mirror, her eyes fell to the speedometer. He was keeping the car at a reckless 55 mph, a speed totally unsuited to these narrow twisting lanes.

'Keith,' she said in a small voice.

He glanced at her. 'Mmm?'

Her heart was beating so hard that she thought she might be sick. Forcing her panic down she said, 'Would you mind slowing down a little, please?'

He eased off the accelerator. 'Sorry, didn't realise. So used to motorway driving, see.'

In all, the six mile drive back to Shepham took just under twenty minutes.

The familiar streets, plus the knowledge that she would soon be alone again, eased Laura's fears slightly. Following her directions, he soon had the car parked outside the small Chiltern cottage.

After he switched off the engine, the silence grew thicker, and more ominous.

'This is it, then, is it?' he asked, peering through the windscreen at the moon-washed house.

'Yes.'

Before he could say more, she opened the door and got out of the car. Almost at once, the night air cleared her head a little.

He, too, vacated the car, then came around the front to peer down at her. 'That better?' he asked.

'Yes, thank you.' She took the keys from him and slipped them quickly into her purse, almost as if she were afraid he might suddenly snatch them back again. She felt nervous, and anxious for him to go.

'Well, thanks for driving me home, Keith. It really was very kind — '

He glanced at his watch. 'Hey, it's only twenty past nine now. The night's still young. How about a coffee for your knight in shining armour?'

She felt a stab of panic re-surfacing. Touching her head she said, 'Well . . . '

'Go on — then I'll catch the bus back.' He looked along the sleeping lane. 'Buses *do* run through Shepham, I take it?'

'Ye — '

'Okay,' he smiled, taking her arm and leading her up the path to the cottage door before she could offer any form of protest. 'One quick coffee and I'll be on my way, then. Thanks.'

Once inside the house Laura felt even more trapped. But maybe she was over-reacting. Perhaps the build-up to the party and then the let-down that came as soon as she'd walked through the door had served to make her hypersensitive. And her blinding head-ache certainly wasn't helping matters, either.

Where was the harm in a cup of coffee, anyway? Really, she should have thought to offer him that much herself. It was the least she could do, bearing in mind his kindness . . .

If it *was* kindness . . .

Keith was standing in the middle of the living room with his hands in his pockets, studying the ornaments, pictures and books on display.

'Nice place you've got,' he commented, turning to look her straight in the face. 'Live alone, do you?'

Laura's eyes shifted away from his, then came back. 'No,' she said, hoping that her tone would not betray the lie. 'No, I have two friends. We . . . we share. I couldn't possibly afford a place like this on my own.'

He nodded.

'I'll . . . I'll go and make the coffee,' she said, turning away.

When she was almost through the doorway he said, 'Where are they now, then?'

She turned and stared at him.

'Your two friends,' he explained.

'Oh, out. Be home soon I . . . expect.'

In the kitchen she spooned coffee into a pair of mugs with trembling fingers. He knew she was lying, he *knew*

93

it! And he also knew that she didn't trust him.

The question was: what was he going to *do* about it?

Laura carried the tray into the living room and set it down on an occasional table, trying desperately to behave normally.

'Help yourself to sugar, Keith.'

'Thanks.'

As she retreated to a chair on the other side of the room, she felt his eyes on her. She sat down, feeling as jumpy as a kitten, and sipped her own coffee to moisten her fear-dried lips. Her cheeks were burning and her patience was fast running out. Would this evening never end?

'What do they do?' Keith asked suddenly, showing her his winning smile. 'These two friends of yours, I mean.'

She thought fast. 'One's a graphic artist,' she said evenly. 'The other works for a local estate agent.' To change the subject she said, 'Would you excuse me a moment? I'm afraid I've just got to take a couple of aspirins for this headache.'

'Go ahead,' he invited generously.

Her heart sank. She had hoped that he might take the hint and leave her in peace, but evidently he had no intention of going just yet. She left the room just as the phone began to ring, then turned and took a pace back to answer it.

Salvation!

But he was already beside the phone, smiling. 'You go take your aspirins,' he said softly. 'I'll get this.'

★   ★   ★

The last thing Mark expected to hear was a man's voice. It threw him completely. 'Hello? I'm sorry, I think I may have mis-dialled. I was after four-three-eight-seven.'

'This is four-three-eight-seven,' Keith replied smoothly at the other end of the line. 'Can I help you?'

'I . . . Is Laura there by any chance?'

Keith replied, 'Well she *is* and she *isn't*. That's to say she's outside taking some aspirins at the moment. We went to a party, you see, and she got the most almighty headache. Can I take a message?'

★   ★   ★

There was a long pause. Keith said, 'Hello, are you still there?' He listened for a moment, then smiled into the mouthpiece. 'Sure. I'll tell her. Nice to talk to you, Mark. Bye for now.'

Standing in the living room doorway, Laura watched Keith slowly replace the receiver with a look of disbelief on her face. He said conversationally, 'That was Mark. Sounds like a nice enough fellow. Said he'd call you back tomorrow.'

Laura barely heard him. Her eyes remaining on his smooth, dark features, she reached a decision. The time for pretence was over. On both sides.

'I think you'd better leave,' she said quietly.

He looked injured. 'Leave? Oh come on, Laura. You know you don't mean that.'

Almost as if in a dream she said, 'Yes I do. You had no right to answer that phone — '

'Look, let's not — '

'That's right,' she cut in, her steely voice betraying no fear whatsoever now. 'Let's *not*. Let's not do *anything*.' Their eyes met and locked. 'I've suggested that you leave, Keith. Now I'm *telling* you to.'

The smile slid off his face to be replaced by a look of cold malevolence. He took one pace towards her. He looked very tall and very fit and very strong. 'You're kidding yourself if you think I came all this way just for a lousy cup of coffee.'

With a gargantuan effort Laura stood her ground. 'I'm grateful for all your help,' she said, trying to keep both the situation and herself calm. 'But you can

97

forget whatever it was you thought you could get here. I know it sounds old-fashioned, but it happens to be true. I'm not that sort of girl.'

'That,' he grinned, 'is what they *all* say.'

No sooner were his words in the air than he was upon her, his hands reaching out to pin her arms to her sides.

They struggled for a moment, he growling, she moaning as his grip increased. She tried desperately to pull away, but he was too strong for her. Then, lashing out in blind panic, one of her kicks caught his shin.

As the pain speared up his leg he gave a yelp and released his hold on her. Immediately she stumbled back out of his reach, sobbing.

He came at her again, but this time she was ready for him, and it was she who struck first, raking her nails down his unprotected face.

'*Aaagh!*'

That halted his advance at once. His

hands went up to the line of blood-beads marking his cheek, and he swore.

She retreated even further out of reach, trembling not so much with fear anymore but with anger that he should have tried to violate her.

'*Get out of here!*' she yelled. 'Get out of here now and be grateful that I don't take this any further!'

His lip curled. 'You — '

'Do it *now*,' she gasped.

He stood there a moment longer, until a thin trickle of blood dripped down onto his shirt. Then he edged around the room, almost as if he were afraid of her, and backed along the shadowy hallway towards the front door.

She stood rooted to the spot, following him with her eyes. Then he came up hard against the door and reached behind him for the handle.

'You'll be sorry for this,' he whispered. 'Maybe not today, or tomorrow, or next week. But one day.'

Then he was gone, slamming the

door behind him.

For long seconds she stood where she was. The only things that moved were the tears streaming down her cheeks.

⋆   ⋆   ⋆

The Shepham branch of Barber & Jennings stayed open between ten and four each Sunday, during which time the office was manned by a skeleton staff. On that particular Sunday morning, the staff comprised a very introspective Mark and an equally subdued Sarah.

Business that day had been slack, almost certainly due to the fact that they were now well into the holiday season. Apart from catching up on a few odd jobs, neither of them was kept fully occupied — which, Mark felt, was perhaps just as well, since his mind wasn't on his job at all, and Sarah didn't appear to be any more enthusiastic.

After a long, uncomfortable morning, the hands of the wall-clock finally crawled around to three o'clock. The end of the working day was finally in sight. With little sign of further custom, Mark decided to close up shop for the day.

As they gathered their things together, he asked, 'What have you got planned for this afternoon, then?'

'Oh, the usual,' Sarah said vaguely.

'And what's that, exactly?' he enquired as they stepped out into quiet, sunny High Road and turned to lock up.

'Go home, have lunch, do the dishes, maybe go for a walk,' she said mechanically.

'Sounds nice.'

'If you've got someone to share it with,' she murmured. 'How about you?'

'Much the same as you, I expect.'

She fell silent for a moment, then said, 'Mark — say no if you want to. Don't worry, I won't be offended. But . . . well, it seems silly to cook lunch for one when you could just as easily cook it for two.'

He hesitated before replying.

'I mean, I've got more than enough

101

to go around back at the flat,' she said.

She looked and sounded so keen that he hated to disappoint her.

So that was how they came to spend the late afternoon eating salad and drinking wine at Sarah's impressively modern flat, with the sun pouring across the silver and teak of picture frames and dining table.

'I come from a large family,' Sarah said as she toyed with her food. She'd already accounted for two glasses of *Fleur d'Alsace*, and was relaxing by the minute. 'Well, four brothers and me, which I suppose is quite large by today's standards.

'I had a very happy childhood. I grew up in and around Alfort. We weren't a particularly close family, but there was always a certain warmth between us. I love them all a great deal. But . . .' She shrugged. 'There was always something nagging at the back of my mind — not that I was a disappointment to my parents because I was a girl, that's too much of a cliché — but as if I were somehow in *competition* with my brothers the whole time. That's why I grew up to be so ambitious, I suppose.'

Seeing his expression, she chuckled. 'Oh, don't worry, I know I can be a bit overpowering. Pompous, even. But that's because even now I feel that I have to *prove* myself. I *have* to. It doesn't matter what it is I'm doing — I have to play to win.' She looked directly at him. 'Is that awful, do you think?'

He shook his head. 'There's nothing wrong with wanting to succeed,' he allowed.

'That's what I think, too,' she agreed. 'So I worked hard at school and came away with an armful of qualifications, and I went to college and received commendations for performance in business studies, and I left home, got a place of my own here and came to work for you.'

She stopped suddenly, her face uncomfortably serious in the pale sunlight highlighting the copper curls atop her head. 'But when you get right down to it,' she said, 'What have I really got?' She shook her head. 'Nothing.'

He felt he should say something to the contrary. 'You're wrong, Sarah. Look at what you've already told me. You come from a good, caring family. You've got a job — which, I must say, you do very well indeed. And you've got this place. How many other girls of your age can say that?'

But she didn't seem especially impressed by his speech. 'Oh yes,' she said. 'I've got all that. But what's the use of any of it if you've no-one to share it with? No friends, not even a casual acquaintance. No-one.'

He frowned. 'I don't — '

'I'm all alone, Mark,' she said helplessly. 'I'm surrounded by people, and yet I'm all alone. At school I studied all the hours God sent. At college I was the same. I never allowed myself any time to make friends, and I guess that endless *drive* of mine scared away the few friends I *did* have.'

She took another sip of wine from the glass beside her. 'So,' she said bitterly. 'What price, success, eh?'

He had no answer. But suddenly he saw her in a new and sympathetic light.

'Well,' she said, smiling. 'Thanks to this excellent *Fleur d'Alsace*, I've opened up to you. I can't say whether or not it's done me any good, but I feel better for having shared it with someone.' Her eyes fastened on him. 'Your turn.'

'Eh?'

'What is it that's eating at *you?*'

His automatic response was to say, 'Nothing.' But almost as soon as he said it, some sudden, indefinable compulsion made him *want* to tell her the truth.

It occurred to him that maybe *he* was a little drunk, too.

'Actually, my trouble's pretty straight-forward, really,' he said, embarrassed and trying to make light of it. 'I'm in love with a girl who doesn't even know it. And worse, just as I made up my mind to tell her how I felt, I found out that she's already got a boyfriend I didn't know anything about.'

Sarah eyed him steadily. 'Laura,' she said.

He didn't catch the ice in her tone.

'Yes,' he nodded. 'Silly, isn't it? I mean, I'm not even sure exactly when I first realised . . . how I felt. But how do you tell someone you've known all your life that they mean more to you than . . . than perhaps they should?

'Anyway,' he sighed, 'I finally decided that the best thing I could do was speak to her about it, get it all out in the open and settle the matter one way or the other. But when I phoned her last night — '

Sarah set down her glass. ' — her boyfriend answered the call?'

'Yes.'

She rose and came across to sit on the arm of his chair. 'Poor old Mark,' she said with feeling. 'Tying yourself up in knots over someone who's already spoken for.'

He wasn't sure that giving voice to his own problems had made him feel better or worse. Maybe some sense of relief or release would come later.

'Listen to me, Mark,' Sarah said intensely. 'Listen to me because believe it or not, I know exactly how you feel.'

Catching his glance she said, 'Yes, I'm in love with someone who's all wrapped up in someone else, too. But I'll never give in to gloom and despondency, Mark, and neither should you. You've got to find the determination and strength to carry on. You've got to forget the people you want but can never have, put them out of your mind. You've got to convince yourself that, somewhere down the line, there'll be someone *else* for you — '

In the instant before they kissed, he realised without wanting to realise that she was talking about him, that *he* was the one she wanted.

But then the kiss ended all further thought.

He knew it was wrong. He knew *he*

was wrong. But the wine had blurred his thinking.

As her fingers knitted themselves in his thick sandy hair, so his arms went around her, gliding across the warm, silky back of her plain white blouse to pull her closer.

Their kiss was long and intimate. They were so close that each could feel the burning heat emanating from the other. But although there was fervour to the kiss, there was no true desire.

Eventually they slowly drew away from each other, each of them slightly breathless. Their eyes met, slipped away to focus on other, safer targets. Then Sarah stood up, smoothed down her skirt with the same brisk efficiency he always associated with her, and he too rose to his feet.

'Sarah, I'm sorry, I — '

But she put a long-nailed finger to his lips to indicate that he should say no more. 'Don't be sorry, Mark. You've nothing to feel sorry for. I love you. I've been in love with you for months now, *months*. And I'll resign, if it makes things any easier for you,' she said. 'I mean, I *will* anyway, now that I've actually told you how I feel.'

'Of course you won't,' he said. He stepped forward and took hold of her by the shoulders. 'I appreciate your honesty, Sarah. And believe it or not, I've appreciated this opportunity for us to talk. But I won't hear any more talk of resignation.'

She looked up into his troubled blue eyes. 'But — '

His thinking still impaired by the wine, he said, 'We'll work this out, somehow. Maybe we'll even . . . you know, give it a try. You and me, together.'

'Oh, Mark . . . '

She pressed herself to him, crushing one side of her face into his shoulder.

And in that way he failed to see the smile that played across her mouth — a smile of triumphant satisfaction.

6

On Monday, when Karen Kingsley dropped in and found out what had happened between Laura and Keith on Saturday night, she couldn't apologise enough.

'It's all right,' Laura interrupted as the younger girl grew more and more agitated. 'It wasn't your fault.'

'Yes, it was,' Karen insisted. 'You were right all along. I should never have forced you to come with me. They weren't a very nice crowd at all. I didn't know half of them myself. And I certainly shouldn't have left you on your own the way I did. I guess I just got carried away.'

Laura reached out to put a hand on the teenager's arm. 'Don't worry about it. It's all over now, and there was no harm done.'

Karen eyed her closely. 'You're sure?'

'Of course I am.'

'If I thought for one moment — '

'Karen, I'm all right.'

'Still friends, then?' the teenager asked ruefully.

Laura's smile made the girl relax a little. 'Yes,' she replied. 'Still friends.'

But she couldn't deny that her entire weekend had been a very unpleasant experience. She hadn't slept a wink on Saturday night, and had been unable to face food all day Sunday. Upon venturing outside on Sunday morning to park the car in the drive, and off the road where Keith had left it, she had discovered a ragged line running the length of one side of the Polo which had been gouged with a pen-knife or key or some other sharp object, and the tears had returned hot and stinging to her eyes.

She wanted to believe that Keith was gone. But remembering the absolute certainty of his parting shot — *You'll be sorry for this. Maybe not today, or tomorrow, or next week. But one day*

111

— she had a nasty feeling that, sooner or later, he was going to turn up again, and when she least expected it.

* * *

A week or so later, Laura finally gave up trying to find herself a job. The endless stream of rejections was just too discouraging.

Instead, she drove into Colbury and signed on at an employment agency, and they found her some general reception work at a local fabric printing company. But five weeks later the company lost a valuable overseas order, and was forced to make immediate savings, particularly in staff.

'Last in, first out,' she was told not unkindly by the office manager. 'I'm sorry, Laura, that's just the way it's worked out. But if you ever need a reference, don't hesitate to put my name down.'

She accepted the loss without complaint, but as she left work for the last time one chilly Friday evening, she couldn't help but feel her spirits drop. She'd grown to like the independence work had brought to her life, and didn't intend to give it up without a fight. Her first priority now was to find a position elsewhere, but it looked as if she would have to wait until Monday morning before she could start job-hunting again.

It was at that moment that she spotted two familiar faces, and almost at once forgot her troubles. Injecting some lightness into her tone, she said, 'Hello there!'

Unaware of her presence, Derek and Shirley Barber had been engaged in conversation. From the number of bags the unsmiling Derek was carrying, it appeared that Shirley had been on another of her infamous shopping sprees.

Now Mark's parents broke off to face the source of the greeting. In the instant that Shirley recognised her, warmth sprang into her eyes. Derek's parchment face, on the other hand, showed only irritation at the interruption.

'Laura!' Shirley gave her a hug. 'My goodness, where did you spring from? We haven't seen you in ages.'

Laura explained that she'd just come from work, and was sorry that even now their meeting had only come about by chance.

'Where are you off to?' asked Shirley.

'Home.'

'Why don't you come with us? We were just going into Lettieri's for coffee.'

Immediately Laura's eyes shuttled to Derek, whose animosity towards her was every bit as obvious now as it had been on the afternoon of her mother's funeral. What was it he had against her? She had never knowingly done anything to offend him. Why did he dislike her so much?

'Good, that's settled then,' Shirley went on, sensing the coolness between them but glossing over it with her usual tact. 'Come on, I'm famished!'

At this time of day Lettieri's opened

to provide a light refreshment service to shoppers before the evening trade began. Inside, the atmosphere was warm and friendly, but as they settled into a booth near the entrance, Derek's mood remained stubbornly frozen.

'I didn't know you'd found a job,' Shirley commented once Derek had given a hovering waiter their order. 'What are you doing?'

'Well, nothing grand. General office duties, I suppose you'd call it.'

'Well, I'm sure it's very interesting. Who are you working for?'

'Hill and Spencer.'

'The cloth manufacturers?'

'Yes.'

'I heard they're having money troubles,' Derek cut in suddenly. 'Serious ones. Laying off a lot of staff.'

He appeared to relish the dismal prospect.

'That's right,' Laura replied evenly. 'In fact, you could say I was the first casualty.'

Shirley tilted her blonde head to one

side and assumed a look of sympathy. 'Oh, I *am* sorry, Laura. You can't have worked there all that long, either.'

'Just long enough to realise how much I enjoyed it,' Laura replied. 'Still, I intend to start job-hunting again on Monday.'

'That's the spirit.'

After the waiter delivered their order, Laura asked what had brought them to Colbury.

'Oh, just one of her usual spending sprees,' Derek replied sourly before Shirley could open her mouth.

'What he means,' Shirley went on with a patient glance at her dour husband, 'is that I've been invited to a Rotarian function in two weeks' time and we've been out trying to find the right outfit for the occasion.'

'So she's bought half a dozen just to make sure she's got a choice when the time comes,' Derek complained.

The two women laughed politely, although there had been no trace of humour in Derek's tone.

After coffee, and just before Laura left them alone, Shirley made what was to be a prophetic suggestion.

'If you find yourself stuck for a job, Laura, why don't you have a word with Mark?'

Laura shook her head. 'Oh, I couldn't. He might feel obliged — '

'You *could*,' Shirley insisted good-naturedly. 'In fact, between you and I, he'd probably welcome an extra pair of hands at the moment. He's rushed off his feet, poor boy.'

'Well . . . '

'I'll mention it to *him* if you'd prefer,' Shirley said helpfully.

'That's if you can pin him down,' Derek grunted. 'You know what he's been like ever since he started going out with Sarah Clarke — here, there and everywhere.'

Shirley darted him a silencing glance. 'Exaggerating again,' she remarked.

'Am I?' Derek asked. Once more his blood-shot eyes fairly burned into Laura. 'Mind you, I'm not complaining.

117

As far as I'm concerned, she's been the best thing for him, that girl. Really brought him out of his shell.'

Laura fought the urge to fidget. 'That's good,' she replied, trying to sound sincere but for some reason finding it difficult. 'And thank you for thinking of me, Shirley.'

'Nonsense. I'm sure we can sort something out,' Shirley said warmly, trying to make up for Derek's plain bad manners. 'I'm so glad we ran into each other, Laura. Let's not leave it so long next time, eh?'

They embraced, and with a civil nod to Derek, Laura eased out of the booth and left the restaurant. As they watched her go, Derek turned his short-tempered gaze onto his wife, his anger barely suppressed.

'What do you mean, 'Why don't you have a word with Mark?' The boy's running an estate agency, not a charity!'

If Shirley took offence at his words, it didn't show. 'Laura wants a job,' she explained simply. 'Mark's got a vacancy.

Why shouldn't I try to help them both get what they want?'

Derek gave a derisive snort. 'How do *you* know what Mark wants?' he asked sarcastically.

His wife's gaze cooled toward him. 'How do *you*?'

Instead of replying directly, he muttered, 'I can't see why she needs to work, anyway. Can't she get by on what we pay her every month?'

Shirley twisted around so that she could appraise him more directly. It seemed that the time for straight talking between them had arrived at last. 'The money *we* pay her,' she explained, ''*we*' being the company of which her father was a co-founder, is an allowance, Derek, a very modest *allowance*. But you *are* right in one respect. She doesn't need to work — but she *wants* to. Can't you see that?'

He hurriedly finished the dregs of his black, unsweetened coffee.

'What have you got against Laura, Derek? You used to think the world of her when she was a little girl.'

'Stop nagging me, woman.'

'No, Derek. We really need to talk about this. Now — what is it about Laura?'

He gestured emptily with one hand. 'Her and Mark,' he said grudgingly.

'What about them?'

'Can't you see the boy's besotted with her?'

'I'd hardly say that.'

'It's obvious.'

'Well what if it is? He could do a lot worse.'

'And he could do a lot *better*,' Derek retorted. 'Mark has a bright future ahead of him, but if he saddles himself with the likes of Laura Jennings — !'

'Derek!'

'Well, tell me otherwise, then, if I'm so wrong. If she's anywhere as weak and neurotic as her mother was — '

'She *isn't*.'

'How do you *know*?' He shook his head in agitation. 'If he *must* find a wife, he should pick one who'll be good for his career, someone who'll support him through good times and bad, someone with a bit of character, who'll be good for him *and* the business.'

'Is that why you picked me, then?' Shirley asked. 'Because you thought I'd be good for *your* career?'

'Oh, you know what I'm trying to say.'

'No, Derek, I don't. I *really* don't.' Angrily she gathered up her things. 'Now, come on — one more store to look at, and then we'll call it a day.'

★   ★   ★

Laura's Polo was parked in a multi-level car park ten minutes' walk from the Hill & Spencer building. As soon as she reached it she unlocked the still-scratched driver's door, climbed inside, closed the door behind her, started the engine and turned up the heater. The evening was cold — it was only September, autumn was already on the way.

As she prepared herself for the drive

home, her thoughts returned to Shirley and Derek. How could two people be so different, and yet have a marriage which had survived more than thirty years? Perhaps it really *was* true about opposites attracting. Take Mark and Sarah, for example —

But for some strange and sudden reason she didn't care to pursue that line of thought. Somehow she didn't like to think of Mark spending his time with someone like Sarah Clarke. It was irrational, of course, but she continued to find the idea oddly annoying.

Anyway, it was nothing to do with her, and in any case she had other things to occupy her mind now, such as finding another job. And it was hardly fair to judge Sarah Clarke so harshly after just one meeting.

She stared through the windscreen at the drab stone wall and parked cars opposite, distracted momentarily. The thoughts that now came to mind were unbidden, unwelcome, but stubbornly persistent.

Mark and Sarah . . .

Her gloved hands clenched the steering wheel tighter. What was the matter with her? She should be happy for Mark, and happier still for Sarah, that she had found such a warm and intelligent and above all *caring* young man —

Suddenly she stiffened in her seat and a hot tingle washed across her face.

There was that word again.

Man.

That was when she recognised her sudden restlessness as a symptom of jealousy.

But surely . . . she shook her head, confused and unsettled. *I mean, we're practically brother and sister . . .*

The insistent little voice at the back of her mind had other ideas, however. *No*, it replied. *You are nothing of the sort.*

Suddenly she wanted to be home, surrounded by familiar, comforting things. She wanted to be alone to think, sort out her unexpected and blinding bewilderment and understand this sudden storm of emotions.

She slipped the car into first gear and pulled away from her parking space abruptly, leaving only a wail of protesting brakes behind her.

* * *

'I'm sorry, Mark, but I'm just not prepared to go on working in this sort of atmosphere. Spying on me, criticising me . . . ' Bill Everett took his grey eyes away from the hands fidgeting in his lap long enough to peer straight into his employer's concerned face. 'I'm sorry, mate. It's just not on.'

It was very quiet in the small office once he'd finished his outburst.

Mark digested what the other man had said, and nodded his understanding. Bill Everett had been an estate agent for more than half his forty-two years and he knew the business backwards. In the eight years he had worked for Barber & Jennings, Mark had always found him to be loyal and conscientious. So to see him so distraught now did nothing to improve Mark's rainy Monday morning.

'Well,' he said in a sigh. 'First of all, let me set your mind at rest, Bill. As far as I'm concerned, you're doing as good a job now as you've ever done. I've no complaints at all. And as for the somewhat erratic hours you've been putting in lately — '

Bill opened his mouth to speak, but Mark raised one hand for silence.

'I'd be a pretty hard man if I didn't understand and sympathise with what lay behind them,' he finished.

Bill Everett relaxed.

'Now, I don't like talk of resignation, particularly when it comes from someone I value highly and don't want to lose. But I can quite understand your position. So let me put it this way. I'm not blind. I know things around here have changed a bit lately, and I'm as keen as you to get them back to how they were. So just forget all this talk of resignation and give me a chance to sort everything out.'

Bill looked visibly relieved. 'Sure, Mark. But . . . I don't like to put you in a spot like this.'

'You're not putting me in a spot, Bill. Honestly. As far as I'm concerned, you deserve a bonus for bringing the matter to a head.'

As soon as the office door closed behind the other man, the smile fell off Mark's haggard face. How had he gotten himself into this situation? Things hadn't been the same since that Sunday afternoon at Sarah's flat. Feeling rejected by Laura, even though he knew she wasn't to blame, and feeling sorry for and guilty about Sarah Clarke, he had eventually come to find himself occupying the position of Sarah's boyfriend. And to be fair, once or twice he had actually enjoyed himself on their many trips out.

But there was nothing inside him for Sarah Clarke, no feelings save those two basic emotions of pity and guilt.

So enough, he decided, was enough.

He got up, moved around the desk and peered outside. 'Sarah, could I have a word, please?'

He had just resumed his seat when she entered his office and closed the door behind her. She looked stunning in a warm brown skirt and matching jacket. There was no other word for her.

'Yes, Mark? Was it something about the de Masi concert in Alfort tonight?'

'No, it's more important than that. And it concerns work.' She frowned at the tone of his voice and sat down slowly. 'Specifically,' he said, 'it's about Bill Everett.'

'All right,' she replied coolly. 'I'm listening.'

'It appears that you've been telling him what he should and shouldn't be doing,' Mark said quietly, keeping his tone neutral. 'You've also been clock-watching him.'

She nodded. 'That's right,' she replied. 'His time-keeping's atrocious. I merely brought the fact to his attention.

As for anything else I may have mentioned to him — such as the vast amount of time he spends on each of his clients — yes, I've picked him up on that, too.'

Mark eyed her steadily. 'But you seem to be forgetting something, Sarah.'

She lifted one eyebrow above the rim of her glasses. 'Which is . . . ?'

'It's not your job to do that.'

'But — '

He leaned forward across the desk. 'Listen to me, Sarah. Bill Everett is a first-class worker and I value him highly. Each of us works in his or her own way. As far as Bill is concerned, I don't care how much time he spends with his clients as long as he continues to get results — which he does.'

Again she tried to interrupt, but he kept talking. 'And as for his time-keeping, I've just told him that he can put in as many, or as few, hours as he likes until his wife has their baby.'

'But Mark — '

'Hear me out, Sarah. Please.'

She fell silent.

'Now — I don't know whether or not you're aware of the situation, but Bill and his wife have been trying to start a family for years. Up till now all they've had are miscarriages, three of them, so this time they're leaving nothing to chance.'

He looked straight through the grey lenses of her glasses and into her wide blue eyes. 'When Bill isn't here, he's racing around trying to do as much as he can to help his wife, so as far as I'm concerned, he can keep whatever hours he likes if that's what it takes to help them have a healthy baby. Do I make myself clear?'

They locked stares for five long seconds, during which her mouth thinned down and something in her eyes grew hard.

'Yes, I understand,' she said, maintaining her cool tone. 'But it doesn't look very good when you go around undermining my authority, you know.'

He stared at her, incredulous. '*Authority?*' he echoed. 'What authority?'

'As office manager,' she explained.

Now he was thoroughly confused, and more than a little angry. 'I think I must have missed something,' he decided. 'Just when did you assume this mythical position?'

Her reply dripped venom. 'I've been doing it for about a month,' she said. 'I thought you might have *noticed* by now.'

'The only thing I've noticed is the feeling of frustration and resentment building up among my staff,' he shot back. 'Look, I think we'd better get something straight, Sarah. Your position here is basically that of receptionist. And that's all. As you know, it was always my intention to train you up to full agent status, but beyond that nothing has changed. You've received no form of up-grading or promotion whatsoever.'

'But you said — '

He shook his head. 'I never said a

word, Sarah, and you know it.'

'But we discussed it one evening about a month ago,' she persisted. 'About how this place would run so much better if it had an office manager — '

'That's right,' he agreed, silencing her. 'But that's *all* it was, a *discussion*. You had no right to take on any such role, and certainly no business assuming seniority over Bill Everett.'

Her voice was high and petulant now. 'But I naturally assumed — '

'Exactly,' he interrupted. 'You naturally assumed that because we were seeing each other on a social level, you could do anything you wanted here at work.' He stood up. 'Well, I'm sorry, Sarah. You were wrong.'

The office seemed warm, stuffy, full of tension.

'Now,' he said, trying hard to keep the irritation out of his voice, 'I don't like any form of unpleasantness. None of us does. But I hope this clears the matter up once and for all.'

131

She stood up. 'Oh, it does,' she replied evenly. 'Perfectly.'

As she turned to leave him alone, he read something more into her last word and lifted his hand. 'Sarah — '

The only reply was the door closing behind her.

He sat down again, not altogether sorry that she had chosen to end their relationship. It had run its course anyway, as far as he was concerned.

He took out his pen to tick that last unpleasant task off his list. Once the pen was in his hand he paused to look at it. It had been a present from Laura.

He smiled. Somehow, everything always came to back to Laura. Because he had promised his mother that he would give her a call today. That was his next task.

His eyes travelled to the telephone. He'd lost count of the times he'd stared at that instrument, running her number through his mind. But now, although his heartbeat quickened slightly just at the prospect of talking to her, part of him wanted to avoid, or at least delay, the conversation.

Still, he'd promised his mother . . .

He sighed and picked up the phone.

★   ★   ★

Laura was up in her bedroom when the phone started ringing. She was just slipping into a coat before driving back into Colbury on the job-hunting trip she'd promised herself on Friday evening. But part of her had been expecting this call, just as part of her was not at all sure that she should answer it.

'H — hello?'

It was him.

'Hello, Laura? Hi, it's Mark. I didn't interrupt anything, did I?'

'No, not at all.'

'Oh, good. How are you?'

Her heart fluttered madly, but she tried to keep her voice causal and light. 'I'm fine. You?'

'Yes, fine.'

There was a long pause.

'Mum tells — '

'I was just — '

Another pause. Then Laura said, 'I'm sorry, I interrupted. You were saying?'

'Well, I was speaking to mum over the weekend, and she tells me you're looking for a job.'

'Well, yes. But — '

'She tells me you were working for Hill & Spencer,' he said. 'Something about general office duties.'

'That's right. I picked up a little bit of typing while I was there, too. Some computer skills.'

'Sounds good.'

'It was.'

'I've got a similar vacancy here,' he said. 'Typing, filing, photocopying, admin. But there's no reason why it should stop there.'

She made no immediate response. But she couldn't help thinking that it would be unwise for her to work with him now, particularly in view of the way she felt about him. And she certainly didn't want to cause any ill-feeling between Mark and Sarah, however indirectly.

So her voice was strangely formal as she said, 'It's very kind of you, Mark, but I wouldn't want you to feel obliged — '

'Hey, come on, Laura. It's *me* you're talking to, not a stranger. If I didn't have the vacancy I couldn't offer it to you, could I?'

But she was insistent. 'No, really, Mark, I — '

Suddenly there was a voice in the background, and he said, 'Hang on just a minute, Laura.'

She waited patiently, only half-listening to the conversation at the other end of the line. Eventually Mark came back to her.

'Hello? Sorry about that. Look, I've got to dash, but think it over. Please. We need someone desperately, Laura. In fact, we need someone more now than ever.'

She frowned. 'Why?'

He sighed into her ear. 'Because Bill Everett just put his head around the door to tell me the latest news.'

'Which is . . . ?' she asked.

'Sarah Clarke just walked out on us.'

7

However reluctant she was to bring herself into regular, close contact with Mark, there was no way Laura could fail to help him now.

As soon as she replaced the receiver she grabbed her bag and left the cottage. She had no idea what had caused Sarah to walk out the way she had, whether it was to do with work or something more personal, but that was not her main concern just then. As she hurried to the office, her only thought was that at last she was being given a chance to help Mark when it appeared that he needed help the most: to be as supportive to him as he had always been to her.

But when she arrived at the office, he was nowhere to be seen.

'I'm afraid he's, ah, he's gone out,' Bill Everett explained awkwardly after greeting her. 'I'm sorry, Laura, I don't know when he'll be back.'

She had already guessed that Mark would go after Sarah and try to make peace, however. That was Mark's way. And as much as the thought of them making up after a quarrel upset her, she hoped for Mark's sake that a reconciliation between them might be possible.

She smiled gently up at Bill and said, 'It's all right. I know a little of what's happened. I was at the other end of the phone when you told Mark that Sarah had . . . well, had left in a hurry.'

Bill returned her smile. 'Oh, you know the score then,' he replied. 'Good — that means I needn't stand on ceremony any more. Here, come on, take your coat off and let me get you a cup of coffee. You're going to be a big help to us, Laura, I'm sure of it. And believe me, we really need a big help around here at the moment.'

Once she was settled in a comfortable chair, Bill indicated his colleague, a younger man in his early thirties with a long, friendly face and lively brown eyes. 'This, by the way, is Trevor Teale.'

The man nodded. 'Just call me Trev,' he said with a smile.

In such an amiable atmosphere Laura could hardly fail to relax. But somewhere at the back of her mind uneasiness and apprehension still lingered. She knew it wouldn't be easy to work alongside Mark, feeling as she did. And if Sarah's walk-out had been the result of some trouble between them and she later came back to the office, Laura felt that her presence might only cause more friction between them.

But when Mark finally got back to the office forty-five minutes later, his first job was to inform his staff — which he saw to his surprise now included Laura — that Sarah would not be returning to Barber & Jennings.

Perched on the edge of what had up until that morning been Sarah's desk, Mark looked somehow relieved as he addressed them.

'I won't go into too much detail,' he

said as he sipped a reviving coffee. 'As you know, any matter concerning staff is confidential. But you all have a right to know that Sarah will *not* be coming back. She made that point quite clear.'

He ran his blue eyes across the three faces before him.

'Whatever else you might think about her, there's no denying that Sarah will be a loss. After all, she was a good worker and she knew her job. So until we're back to full strength, I'm afraid we're all going to be pulling more than our weight. Still — ' and here he lifted a hand to indicate Laura, ' — I'm sure we've just acquired a valuable asset in Laura, here.'

Laura blushed fiercely.

'Now,' Mark said, rising, 'back to work. Laura — come into my office a minute and we'll fill in a few forms to get you on the payroll officially.'

When she was close enough he reached out to put a hand on her arm. Again she smelled the warmth of his skin, the spicy scent of his aftershave.

But she couldn't bring herself to look into his eyes for any length of time, although she did study him long enough to realise that he didn't seem especially upset by Sarah's sudden departure.

Did that mean his relationship with her was still intact, then? But surely, if that were so, why had she been so adamant in her refusal to return to work? No doubt Laura would be able to piece everything together in time, but for now she was totally confused.

'I can't tell you how pleased I am to have you on the team at last,' he confided softly. 'I don't know why, but I've always felt you belonged here.'

'It's very kind of you to say so.'

'I mean it,' he insisted. 'Anyway, it looks as if we're going to be rushed off our feet for a while. It happens like that from time to time. But everything will soon settle down again, you'll see.'

At that moment Bill Everett came up. 'Excuse me a moment, Laura. Just a quick word, Mark?'

'Sure.' He turned to Laura. 'Just go on in. I shan't be a minute.'

When they were alone, Bill shuffled his feet awkwardly. 'It's pretty obvious that Sarah wouldn't have walked out of here this morning if I hadn't complained to you about her,' he said worriedly. 'I'm really sorry, Mark. I know that you and she . . . ' He shrugged. 'Well, what I'm trying to say is, I hope that I haven't ruined any — '

'Bill,' Mark cut in to save the other man further embarrassment. 'Don't worry about it. Really.'

But the scene at Sarah's flat had not been very pleasant. She hadn't even invited him inside, so their entire dialogue had been conducted in harsh, discomforting whispers on the door-step.

She didn't say a word at first. She just stood there, glaring at him. She looked strained, grim, angry and determined, but so did he. Finally she said, 'Yes?'

'Can I come in?' he asked softly.

'No.'

His shoulders dropped. 'Sarah, we've got to talk.'

'Have we?' she asked archly. 'I was under the impression that we'd said all there was to say.'

'Don't be ridiculous.'

'All right,' she replied. 'You can say whatever you've got to say right here.'

He was a mild man, slow to anger. He had always favoured reason over argument. But she had fanned the flames of his ire long enough, not just with the events of this morning, but with all the ways she had manipulated his actions over the last several weeks.

'All right,' he said sharply. 'Let's start with a straightforward question, then. Just what did you think you'd accomplish by walking out on us the way you did?'

Her shrug was insolent. 'It made you run after me, didn't it?' Defensively she continued, 'I couldn't believe how you treated me just now. Especially in view of the way we feel about each other.'

He shook his head, saying, 'You're confusing business with pleasure. The way I treated you just now was as an employer to an employee. The way it *should* be in matters of business.'

'But you *hurt* me!'

'Sometimes the truth does that to people.'

Her voice was plaintive now. 'Don't you *know* how much I've given to your stupid company?'

'Of course I do,' he said. 'But that isn't the point.'

'Then what is?'

He locked eyes with her. 'You really don't know?' he asked almost pityingly. 'Do you mean to say you couldn't see anything wrong in assuming authority nobody had given you, or cracking the whip over senior members of staff?' He looked earnestly into her face. 'Look — let's not argue. I didn't come here for that. You just made a mistake, Sarah, that's all. You tried to run before you could walk.'

Her full lips curled in a sneer. 'So

that's what it is,' she hissed sibilantly. 'That's what's really behind it all. Jealousy.'

'*What?*'

He could tell by her expression that the bizarre theory appealed to her. 'What is it, then?' she asked mockingly. 'Were you so afraid of my contributions to the business that you thought I'd be after *your* job sooner or later? Is that why you were always so keen to keep me under your thumb?'

Mark shook his head. 'I feel sorry for you if you *believe* that,' he said.

Suddenly the poison left the air. Both of them appeared to deflate, grow weary of the verbal barrage.

'Look,' he said. 'I came here to *talk* to you. I don't want to see you upset. Who would? Yes, you're a good worker, Sarah, and a valuable asset. You just got the wrong end of the stick. Let's not fall out because of that.'

She did not meet his gaze.

'Come on now,' he continued gently. 'Why don't you come back to work with me? This'll all be forgotten in a couple of weeks.'

She searched his face for a long fifteen seconds. 'All right,' she nodded at last. 'But as office manager.'

He stiffened. 'As *receptionist*,' he replied. 'With the promise of training for higher things. Exactly the same as before.'

She shook her head, sending a shiver through her copper curls. 'I'm not coming back on those terms.'

'They're the only terms I'm offering,' he insisted.

'Well, they're not good enough,' she replied. 'Do you think I want to spend my entire life selling seedy little houses in this backwater? I should hope I'm a bit more ambitious than that.' Her voice rose, solidified. 'I think I've had enough of you for the time being, Mark. Go on, get out of my sight.'

They continued to stare at each other for another few seconds, and then he turned away, a number of things suddenly becoming clear to him. He took two steps before she called his name.

He turned to look at her.

'I love you,' she whispered, clutching the doorframe pathetically.

Mark's look was steady and unwavering. 'No, you don't,' he replied, realising that his original conviction that Sarah was a predator and that he was her prey had been correct all along. 'You just see me as a means to an end. A stepping-stone. You're just trying to manipulate me to get where you really want to go in half the time. I see that now.'

'No!' she breathed.

But he could see he was right by the look in her eyes.

'Goodbye, Sarah,' he said. 'And though you probably don't believe me, I wish you luck in the future. Because if you don't curb some of that ambition of yours, and *soon*, I've got a feeling you're going to need it.'

★ ★ ★

As September gave way to October, Laura began to learn her father's business well.

Mark had warned her that she would be thrown in at the deep end. Bill Everett had called it more of a baptism by fire. But although the work was hard and demanding, it brought her enormous satisfaction.

In next to no time she was handling most of the agency's correspondence, fixing and reshuffling appointments, negotiating with the local papers for advertising space and dealing with all sorts of enquiries from property buyers and sellers alike. The job was everything she could ever hope for. But —

But then there was Mark.

He was every bit as kind and generous as an employer as he was a friend. No task or question was too much trouble for him. As a teacher he was second to none. But the barrier he set up between them worried her.

For one thing, he rarely allowed them to be left alone together, almost as if he were uncomfortable in her company, and with the exception of the usual polite conversation, he never asked how she had adjusted to life on her own, or how she filled her free time. It was almost as if he didn't want to hear the answers.

Perhaps it was the fact that he was no longer seeing Sarah Clarke that had changed him, but somehow Laura always sensed that the end of that particular relationship had come as more of a relief than anything else.

Whatever lay behind his somewhat distant manner towards her, she found it both puzzling and upsetting. If it was something about *her* that was worrying him, she would have preferred that he come out and say so. But how could she broach the subject herself when she too was trying to keep their association on a very proper basis?

Sometime during the second week in October he took her on a tour of the company's five branches. Although the day was overcast and eye-wateringly cold, she had a very interesting time. At one o'clock they had lunch at an olde-worlde inn just outside Alfort, but even here, in such warm and pleasant surroundings, he remained curiously aloof.

She passed no comment, however, and at the end of the day, with the countryside shrouded in darkness, he drove her back to the cottage in a more companionable silence.

'Will you come in for tea or coffee?' she asked when he drew up outside her home. Part of her hoped that he would — even as part of her hoped that he wouldn't.

He didn't look at her. 'No. Ah, no thanks, Laura. Better get along.' He glanced at her, then. 'I expect you've got other things to do, anyway.'

There was something in the way he said it that made her frown.

'Going out anywhere nice tonight?' he asked.

She continued to peer at him, sensing that whatever had prompted such a question was also behind his odd treatment of her. She tried in vain to fathom exactly what it was.

'No, nowhere,' she said at last.

'Oh.'

She released the catch and opened the Hyundai's silver-grey door. 'Thanks for the guided tour, Mark. I really enjoyed it. See you in — '

She broke off so suddenly that his head whipped around to see what the matter was. Then he, too, froze.

The front door of the cottage was ajar.

As he slid out from behind the steering wheel and into the crisp, still air, they were both thinking the same thing: *Burglars? Had she been burgled?*

'Mark?'

He placed one gloved hand on her arm but never took his eyes from the dark, shadowy cottage. 'Were you expecting visitors?' he whispered back. 'Did you give your key out to anyone?'

'No.'

'All right — stay here.'

Followed by her anxious gaze, he advanced upon the cottage and pushed the door all the way open. Laura heard the small, tired creaking of the hinges. Mark disappeared inside.

She waited. And waited.

Eventually she could stand it no more. Anything might have happened to him. With her fingers still knitted in front of her, she threw caution to the wind and ran up the path, the gravel crunching beneath her boots.

There was a light on in the living room. She hurried towards it, praying that he was all right, that no harm had come to him.

Mark appeared in front of her and grabbed her by the arms. 'All right, all right, calm down . . . '

'What . . . what's — ?'

She struggled, but he held her firm. 'Don't go in there.'

'But — '

Somehow she escaped his strong hands and rushed past him into the room. She pulled up short and gasped.

The living room was a shambles. It looked as if a hurricane had swept through it. Every ornament that could be smashed *had* been. Every picture had been ripped to shreds, as had the sofa and chairs. The carpet was strewn with debris, and on the mantelpiece was a card upon which had been scrawled:

I TOLD YOU YOU'D BE SORRY.

Without consciously realising it, she loosed a tortured moan and as her legs weakened beneath her she turned and fell into Mark's strong arms.

As he pulled her to him and whispered words of comfort, her body was wracked by a series of piteous sobs. His hands held her tight, his presence gave her strength. She reached out and pulled him even closer.

'There, there,' he said quietly. 'Shhh, now. Don't worry, I'm here. Everything will be all right.'

She wasn't sure how long they spent

standing there amidst the wreckage, their bodies pressed tightly together. It seemed like hours. But at last she stopped crying and allowed him to lead her into the kitchen, which was still mercifully intact.

Seated at the breakfast bar, she watched as he searched the cupboards, found a bottle of brandy and poured her a generous measure.

'Drink this,' he said as he set the glass down in front of her. 'I'm going to have a look upstairs.'

She turned her smudged eyes on him. 'M-Mark. Please. Be . . . c-careful.'

He was back five minutes later. 'It's all right,' he told her. 'The living room was the only one they damaged. Whoever *they* are.'

'How did he . . . get in?' she managed.

'Forced the lock,' he replied shortly. 'I don't suppose it's difficult, if you know what you're doing.'

She sipped her drink as he stared at her.

'Any ideas who it could have been?' he asked gently.

She shook her head.

'Are you sure? What do you suppose that note meant? 'I told you you'd be sorry'.'

No reply.

'All right,' he sighed. 'You just sit here for a while. I'm going to phone the police.'

She looked up at him then. 'No!' Her tone was imploring. 'Please. Not the police.'

He frowned at her. 'Then you *do* know who did it,' he said.

She nodded and turned her gaze back to the kitchen tiles. 'Yes,' she replied in a lost child's voice. 'It was somebody called Keith.'

He narrowed his eyes. 'Your *boyfriend?*'

'Boyfriend?' the word came out heavy with irony.

'The one I spoke to on the phone that Saturday night a couple of months ago,' he explained.

She shook her head, suddenly remembering Mark's phone call — the phone call Keith had intercepted. 'He wasn't my boyfriend,' she said. 'He was *never* my boyfriend.'

Mark could hardly believe his ears. All this time he'd kept his distance from her, believing that . . .

He sat on the stool next to her and took both her hands into his. 'I think you'd better tell me everything,' he said quietly.

She did.

When she was finished, she looked up at him and saw fury in his eyes. His voice was cold and hard and frightening. She had never seen him that way before.

'Where do I find this Keith?' he asked.

She sighed. 'You don't,' she replied. 'All I knew about him was his first name and that he was an accountant. For all I know he was lying through his teeth.'

He put his hands on her shoulders.

The nearness of him made her tingle, despite the disquieting events which had brought them to this moment.

'You fool,' he said without malice. 'Why didn't you tell me all about this when it first happened?' He could see that she was exhausted so he said, 'Oh well, not to worry. Laura?'

She stared into his face.

'Are you *sure* you don't want me to call the police?'

'Yes.'

'But why?'

She shrugged tiredly. 'It wouldn't serve any useful purpose. I could only tell them what I told you. That wouldn't be much for them to go on. Besides which, I feel such a *fool*.'

'But the man's a lunatic! What's to say he won't try something like this again — when you're at home.'

Her voice was distant. 'I just know,' she said.

'But how can you be so sure?'

She shrugged. 'After I raked his face he told me that I'd be sorry. He came back here today to make sure that I was. In his mind he probably thinks that I *am* sorry now.'

She looked up at him and smiled, actually *smiled*.

'But I'm not, Mark. If he came back here and tried to attack me all over again, I'd do exactly the same thing.'

Some time later they began tidying up the mess. By half-past eleven they'd done all they could. Laura would need replacements for virtually everything but the carpet.

At the front door again, Mark said, 'I wish you'd come back home with me, or let me spend the night here.'

She reached forward to touch him, very much aware that the strange barrier he had erected between them had somehow crumbled during the course of the evening. 'I appreciate the thought. But I'll be all right. Really, I will.'

'I'll see about getting a locksmith over tomorrow,' he said. 'He can change the lock on your front door and do something about improving the security of your other doors and windows.'

'Thanks.'

He stepped out into the darkness. 'Sure you'll be all right?' he asked doubtfully.

She smiled. 'Of course.'

'Well, call me if you need me.'

'I will.'

They looked at each other for a long heartbeat, both of them very, very serious. Then he leaned forward and brushed her cheek with his warm lips.

'Take care,' he said.

Her voice was barely audible. 'You too.'

He crunched off down the drive to his car, got in, switched on the engine and headlights, waved once and drove off. Laura watched him go, then went inside and closed and bolted the front door behind her.

As she climbed the stairs to her bedroom a sudden weariness overtook her. Quickly she changed into her nightdress and climbed into bed. When she switched off the bedside lamp, the darkness swallowed her whole. But as she lay waiting for sleep, her thoughts turned to Mark, and how warm and wonderful it had been in his arms, feeling the sweet pressure of his lips against her hair and hearing his voice so close that she could not listen to it without also sensing the warmth of his breath on her skin.

Mark.

It was those memories that helped her through the long winter's night.

8

It was early November, and Mark felt better than he had in months.

But even though he now knew that Laura didn't have a boyfriend, he was still reluctant to go ahead and tell her how he felt about her. To do so could bring them even closer together — or end their relationship once and for all.

Dare he take that chance?

He had long ago accepted that he had little choice in the matter. And if by revealing his love for her he ended up driving her away from him, well, as regrettable as that was, it was better than living in an agony of uncertainty.

But he didn't intend to charge ahead blindly like the bull in the china shop. No, she deserved better than that. So he resolved to choose the right moment and endeavour to express himself to the best of his ability.

The property market, as Laura had quickly discovered, was as seasonal as any other, and with Christmas just around the corner, business had trailed off dramatically during the last couple of weeks.

There were always other jobs to do, however, as Trevor Teale proved at ten o'clock that Tuesday morning, when he left the office to carry out a series of valuations in and around Bathwood.

Since Bill Everett hadn't arrived for work yet, Laura and Mark had the office to themselves, and as far as Mark was concerned, now seemed to be a perfect time for him to sound her out. But before he could begin to steer the conversation in the desired direction, the phone rang.

Laura answered it. 'Good morning, Barber and Jennings. Can I help you?'

Mark, standing in his office doorway, stiffened as her tone changed suddenly, grew urgent.

'Yes, I understand. Okay.' She looked

up and waved him closer. 'All right,' she went on into the mouthpiece. 'Don't worry about it. We'll see you when we see you. And Bill — good luck. We'll be thinking of you.'

As she put the phone down Mark came to stand beside her.

'That was Bill,' she told him quietly. 'He was phoning from the hospital.'

Mark's face blanched. 'What — ?'

'His wife's gone into labour.'

'But . . . but the baby wasn't due for another couple of months.'

'I know,' she replied sadly. 'Apparently Mary hardly slept a wink last night, and this morning she started to get regular contractions. Bill panicked and rushed her to the hospital, and now he's just waiting.'

'Maybe I should go and keep him company.'

'No. I daresay Mary's parents are there with him.'

Mark glanced at his wristwatch. 'If they lose this baby, it'll kill them both,' he said grimly. 'They want a family so badly I don't think they'd ever get over it.'

'I know.'

Ten o'clock became eleven. Eleven became midday. Somehow they passed the time, but their minds and hearts kept straying to Bill and his wife and their tiny, tiny baby. Neither of them needed reminding how much the child meant to Bill. Some days he had spoken of little else.

At twelve-fifteen Mark was called out to visit a shopkeeper who was hoping to expand his business in the New Year and wanted some idea of how much larger premises were going to cost him. Trevor Teale came back in fifteen minutes later, then went out to lunch, leaving Laura to wait all alone. Then, at one o'clock the phone rang again.

Laura snatched it off its cradle. 'Hello, Barber and Jennings, yes?'

She replaced the receiver five minutes later, just as Mark came back in. Slowly he took his overcoat off and came up to her with a question on his face. He glanced at the phone.

'Was that — ?'

She nodded. 'Oh Mark,' she said as tears filled her eyes, 'Bill's wife just gave birth to a bouncing baby boy! Only five pounds four ounces, but . . . ' She choked off.

He stared at her, then muttered, 'A bouncing baby boy . . . ' He swallowed and a smile split his face. 'Oh my God, Laura, they *did* it! They actually *did* it!'

Without even thinking about it they reached out to hug each other, both of them happier for their friend and colleague than either one could say.

'Oh, thank God . . . '

Suddenly they realised just how close they were, and their faces turned slowly so that each was looking straight at the other. He marvelled at the hazel depths of her eyes as she returned his stare levelly. Then, without needing to think about it, knowing instinctively that it was the right thing to do, he lowered his head and she tilted her face up to meet him.

As they melted into each other Laura felt a moment of panic, that perhaps she shouldn't allow this to go any further. But then her arms came up around him even as his slid up across her back, and each pulled the other closer.

In that moment, when the passion of their kiss reached its height, there was something almost desperate in the way they refused to break the embrace, as if, now that the time had finally arrived, neither of them wanted it to end.

And that was why neither of them saw Derek, who just happened to pass the window at exactly that moment.

★   ★   ★

As their lips parted and the real world flooded back over them, Mark and Laura realised exactly what they had done and abruptly let go of each other. It seemed very close in the office, and both of them could feel the heat in their faces.

'I — '

'No, really, I — '

At that moment the phone started to ring, and grateful for the diversion, Laura reached out to answer it. 'Hello, yes? Yes, I'm sorry. This *is* Barber and Jennings. Of course. Hold the line, please.' Somehow she made herself look into Mark's flushed face. 'It's Neil Mackenzie,' she said.

He nodded. 'I'll take it in my office.'

Once he was back at his desk he cleared his throat and picked up the phone. 'Hello, Mark Barber.'

He heard the cool voice of Mackenzie's secretary. 'Hello, Mr Barber. I have Mr Mackenzie for you.'

There was a click, and then Mackenzie's loud, abrasive voice came on the line. 'Barber? I'd just about given up on you.'

Mark frowned. 'I'm sorry?'

'I thought you were supposed to run a pretty slick operation up there. If the time it takes you to answer the phone is anything to go by . . . '

167

Mackenzie had irritated Mark for as long as he had known him. As he had told Laura many months before, the business magnate was a brash and insensitive man who believed that all he had to do to make people do his bidding was snap his fingers. But he tried not to show his dislike for the other man, reminding himself that he had once been an important client and could well become one again.

'I'm sorry about that. Anyway, how can I help you?'

'How do you think?' Mackenzie shot back. 'A few months ago you were interested in having sole representation of all the properties I was building in New Shepham. Still think you can handle it?'

The question caught Mark off-balance. 'Well, yes. But it was such a long time ago I thought you'd gone off to see if you could get a better deal elsewhere.'

'I did,' Mackenzie replied bluntly. 'And now that I've got all the figures, I want to talk to *you* again.'

At last Mark got his mind in gear. 'Okay. When would you like to — '

'This afternoon. Two-thirty sharp.'

'But — '

'Look, I won't mess around, Barber. You either want my business or you don't.'

'Well, of course I want it.'

'See you on site this afternoon, then.'

Mark sighed, rankled by Mackenzie's arrogant manner but determined not to show it. 'All right.'

'Oh, and don't forget a pen. You never know, I might want to sign an agreement there and then. I wouldn't want you to lose out all for want of a biro.'

And so saying, Mackenzie hung up.

Mark put the phone down and went back out to the main office. Laura said, 'Is everything all right?'

'I think so. Mackenzie wants to see me in New Shepham this afternoon. I believe he's ready to sign a deal for our exclusive representation at long last.'

Despite their awkwardness of a few moments ago, Laura now found a genuine smile of pleasure. 'But — Mark, that's wonderful news!'

He gave another distracted nod. 'Yes,' he said without enthusiasm. 'It's exactly what Dad wanted.'

She frowned into his troubled face. 'But not what *you* want?'

He didn't reply directly. 'Will you come with me this afternoon?'

She blinked, taken aback by the suddenness of his request. 'Me?'

'I'll need you there,' he said.

She was confused. 'But . . . why?'

He summoned a smile of his own as Trevor Teale came back from lunch.

'I don't know,' he replied with a shrug. 'I just will.'

★ ★ ★

'Sometimes I just don't understand you, Derek,' Shirley Barber said wearily.

'No,' he replied dourly. 'I don't suppose you do.'

170

They were in their warm, comfortable sitting room, he pretending to read the paper, she watching his weathered profile closely.

After so many years together, she had grown adept at reading the signs and gauging his moods. The way he always threw himself into the day's news, snapped rather than spoke, glared rather than gazed — for Derek they were classic symptoms. Something was definitely bothering him, and she only wanted to know what it was so that she could try to help him. But as usual, he wasn't going to give an inch.

'You're obviously upset about *something*,' she said. 'It's no good denying it, Derek. I *know* you, remember.' She leaned forward in her seat, her expression soft and concerned. 'Why don't you tell me what it is?'

He returned her look for so long that she thought for one moment that he was actually going to open up and confide in her. But then his expression altered subtly and his heavy, bloodshot eyes veiled over.

'It's nothing.'

He went back to reading the paper.

Shirley continued to study him. He had always been a difficult man to live with, prone to black moods during which he was best left alone. But these days he seemed more difficult and moody than ever. If only he would share his worries, allow her to get closer to him — but he wouldn't.

'If it's about that Mackenzie business — '

'It isn't,' he snapped.

Her sigh was soft and shallow and carefully concealed as he turned a page in his newspaper.

'Is it something to do with your health?' she enquired. 'Something about your heart — ?'

He threw the paper to one side with such vehemence that she jumped.

'For God's sake stop going on at me, woman! No, it is nothing to do with my health! No, it's nothing to do with the Mackenzie deal! And above all it's *nothing to do with you!* Satisfied now?'

They looked at each other across the cosy sitting room, both of them as surprised as each other by his tirade. Then Shirley stood up and walked towards the door.

'Shirley — wait a moment — '

She didn't slam the door behind her as she left the room, but closed it softly, and in a way that made him feel even worse.

He slumped back in his chair, a tired fifty-eight-year-old aged before his time, with his fists clenched tightly in a fury he was powerless to vent.

Why couldn't she understand? Why couldn't she see what a drag Laura Jennings was going to be on their son's career if the two of them weren't somehow split up?

He got up and crossed to the drinks cabinet, where he poured himself a large whiskey that was strictly against doctor's orders. *Laura Jennings*. What did Mark see in her, anyway? He'd had the best possible partner in young

Sarah Clarke. Ah, now there was a go-getter. But no, that match — as perfect as it had appeared to him — hadn't lasted. And ever since Laura's cottage had been turned upside down by some mysterious grudge-bearer, she and Mark had grown ever closer.

His fingers whitened about the glass in his hand. Mark and Laura? No, he couldn't allow it to happen. And he wouldn't.

He tossed back half of the fiery liquid in one vicious gulp.

He wouldn't.

★ ★ ★

For the next thirty minutes there was little time to dwell on what had happened just before Mackenzie's phonecall, and Laura was glad. But once things calmed down again, the memory of that breath-taking kiss came back vivid and insistent.

She was not going to allow herself to read too much into it, however. She wanted to think things through and put them into perspective first. After all, it was too much to hope that Mark would feel about her as she did about him.

So she put it from her mind — or at least *tried* to — and while Mark quickly gathered all the relevant paperwork together and hastily rechecked his original figures in readiness for the meeting, she printed out a provisional agreement which would give Barber & Jennings the right to sell, rent or let all the property that comprised New Shepham.

'Of course, Mackenzie will want a much more exhaustive document than this,' Mark explained as he slipped two copies of the agreement into his brief-case. 'But as long as he agrees to the spirit of *this* contract, we're in business.'

After that there was no more time for talk. Because of the short notice Mackenzie had given them, the ten-mile drive to make their two-thirty appointment on time became one mad rush.

'Nervous?' Laura asked as Mark urged the car long a winding, muddy access road.

'A bit,' he replied quietly.

Five minutes later they came to a temporary gatehouse, where he showed some identification and was then allowed onto the site itself. They had made it with five minutes to spare.

This was the first time Laura had seen the new town-in-the-making, and she was immediately impressed by the enormity of the project. The entire 90,000-acre plot was surrounded by a high chain-link fence topped with barbed wire and patrolled at night by security guards with tracker dogs. Houses, shops, warehouses and offices were springing up as far as the eye could see. Everywhere there were lorries, cranes, cement mixers and workmen. Even through the closed windows of the car they could hear the clamour of drills and hammers and the echoing yells of brightly-garbed construction crews.

'It's incredible,' she muttered.

He pulled up in the wide concrete space reserved for temporary visitors and switched off the engine. Theirs was the only vehicle save for a mini-bus which was used to transport workers to and from the site.

'It should be quite something when it's complete,' he agreed, unbuckling his seat-belt.

She continued to focus her attention on the activity beyond the car park even though she was very much aware that his eyes were on her.

'There's no sign of Mackenzie,' he muttered, more for something to say than anything else. 'Typical! I suppose I'd better go see if I can find him.'

He got out of the car, strode across the parking area and disappeared around a pile of cement sacks and coiled cables.

The sudden bleeping of his mobile phone startled her, coming loud and insistent as it did from where he'd accidentally left it on the dashboard.

She reached over to answer it.

'Yes?'

'Oh, could I speak to Mr Barber please?'

Laura recognised the cool, condescending tones of Neil Mackenzie's secretary. 'I'm afraid he isn't here at the moment,' she explained. 'Can I take a message?'

'Probably. I'm afraid that something has come up requiring Mr Mackenzie's urgent attention, so I'm going to have to re-schedule your two-thirty appointment for four o'clock. Will that be all right?'

Remembering the frantic rush to get here on time, Laura suppressed a sigh, and knowing that Mark had no other appointments for the afternoon, said, 'Okay. Four o'clock it is, then.'

'Thanks so much.'

The line went dead.

Laura rang off, then got out of the car, intending to find Mark and tell him the news. The day was grey and chilly, and she hugged her berry-red cotton waxed jacket closer around her as she crossed the car park.

Beyond the cement sacks and coiled cables she found herself confronted by a wide concrete roadway bordered by a jagged forest of half-erected girders. Even at this early stage it was easy to see that this area would eventually form part of New Shepham's ultra-modern shopping precinct. But nowhere could she see Mark.

She walked on a little further, passing a few busy workmen and trying not to acknowledge the occasional wolf-whistles of the construction crews. She turned into a narrow alley between the shells of two buildings and walked its length, hoping to sight Mark there. At the other end, however, there was only debris and a crackling bonfire.

The entire area was now pale beneath harsh floodlights, and gloomy shadows stretched everywhere. Perhaps she should return to the car and wait for Mark there. She turned to retrace her steps and saw a workman entering the alley

179

from the opposite end, pushing a wheel-barrow full of rubbish ahead of him.

As the distance between them shrank, she saw that he was a tall, sturdily-built man between twenty-five and thirty, with dark eyes, a small nose and a wide, smiling mouth. The hair falling from beneath his yellow hard-hat was dark and thick.

She thought, *Oh my God . . .*

It was Keith!

She saw by the change in his expression that he had also recognised her, and he was so surprised that he released his grip on the wheelbarrow, dropping it back to earth with a loud boom that echoed along the dark alley.

'What are you doing here?' he demanded.

There was uncertainty in his eyes and voice: he was wondering how she had managed to find him, never dreaming that their meeting had only come about by chance.

'I asked you a question,' he said through gritted teeth.

'I'm here with my boss,' she replied, struggling to bring her jangled nerves under control. 'We're here to meet Neil Mackenzie.'

'I don't believe you,' he said coldly, coming around the discarded wheelbarrow to block her path with his large body. 'How did you find me?'

Hurriedly she looked from right to left. On both sides there rose walls of brick and metal to block her path and close her in. 'I didn't,' she replied, taking an involuntary step back. 'I didn't even know you were here until just now.'

He shook his head. 'I don't believe you. What did you hope to gain by tracing me, eh?'

Taking a steadying breath she said, 'Let me past.'

'*Answer me!*' he barked.

In the eerie half-light he looked insane, and the scratches she had left along his cheek were still faintly visible. But her voice was level as she said, 'I'm telling you the truth. I didn't deliberately try to trace you and I'm not hoping to gain anything from it. But — '

He halted his slow advance and cocked his head. 'But *what?*'

'But now that we *are* face to face again,' she said, 'I will say this. You broke into my home and wrecked my living room because you wanted to make me feel sorry, didn't you?'

His eyes closed to slits.

'Well, I *was* sorry, Keith. But I was sorry for *you.*'

'You — '

'Don't come any closer,' she warned. 'In fact, now that I know where to find you, you'd better not come anywhere near me or my cottage ever again, otherwise I'll have the police on you!'

His fingers flexed, then folded into fists. 'Think you can threaten me?' he asked mockingly. 'You made a bad mistake, Laura. Whatever it was you thought you could get from me, it just won't wash. I'm not going to give you any money, if it's blackmail you're thinking of trying. There's no proof, just your word against mine.'

He came forward in a series of quick steps, but she kept retreating, always managing to stay just beyond his reach. Then she felt heat on her back and turned to find that she had come out at the far end of the alley again, among dark hills of debris and the roaring bonfire.

'I'm warning you, Keith,' she said, but now her voice did tremble. 'Let me — '

'*Laura!*'

The sound of Mark's voice cutting through the crackling flames made Laura sag a little with relief. Then he appeared just as Keith swung around to face him.

'Laura — are you all right?'

'Yes, Mark!'

The two men looked at each other in the uncertain orange glow for a few seconds, as Laura edged around them to stand at Mark's side. Mark was tall, but Keith was taller, and heavier. Then an expression of recognition came into Mark's face.

'You're Keith,' he said softly.

Suddenly the belligerence vanished from Keith's face. 'Eh? No, you've got it all wrong, pal. My name's Steve Vardy. I was just passing the alley and I saw this girl in the light of the fire, thought she might be a trespasser or something. So I — '

'I recognise your voice,' said Mark. His blue eyes narrowed. 'I thought you were supposed to be an accountant. Or was that *another* lie?'

Laura's voice was urgent. 'Mark — '

But Mark took a pace closer to the other man. 'Now you listen to me, *Keith*, or *Steve*, or whatever your real name is, because I'm only going to say this once. If Laura or I ever set eyes on you again, I'm going to have you arrested. Understand?'

'Eh? But — '

'That note you left for Laura,' Mark went on. 'That would make interesting evidence, I'm sure. What did it say now? 'I told you you'd be sorry'? Well,' Mark pulled himself up to his full height and spoke in a low, menacing tone, 'I'm telling you the same thing *now*.'

When he moved, it was fast: so fast that Laura didn't really see what happened. But she heard the snap of knuckles striking jawbone and Keith stumbled over backwards, his safety helmet flying off into the shadows.

'Do I make myself clear?' Mark asked, standing over him.

Keith mumbled and nodded, holding his chin.

Mark turned and put an arm around Laura's shoulders. He could feel her trembling, and squeezed her reassuringly. 'Come on, Laura. Let's get back to the car.'

★   ★   ★

'Mackenzie's secretary phoned to put your meeting back to four o'clock,' Laura explained as they slowly retraced their steps to the car. The pressure of Mark's arm around her shoulders felt good, and by the time they got back to the car she'd stopped shaking. 'I was trying to find you to tell you.'

'If you'd turned right instead of left you'd have seen a large caravan. That's the visitor's reception,' Mark replied. 'I was in there. But not to worry.'

Back inside the warmth and comfort of the car he peered at her closely. 'Sure you're all right?'

'Yes. Just a bit shaken up.' She glanced at his hand. 'How are your knuckles?'

He smiled ruefully. 'Aching. If the truth was known, I probably hurt myself more than I hurt Keith.'

She put a hand on his arm. 'What would I do without you?' she asked.

Before he could reply his mobile phone bleeped and Mark snatched it up. 'Hello, Mark Barber.'

'Oh, Mr Barber. It's Mr Mackenzie's secretary here. You had an appointment with Mr Mackenzie at two-thirty that we had to postpone until four o'clock.'

Mark blew on his knuckles. 'Yes.'

'Well, I'm terribly sorry but I'm

afraid I'm going to have to cancel the four o'clock appointment as well.'

There was a pause, during which Mark and Laura exchanged exasperated glances.

'I wonder if we could set something up for the second week in January?' the secretary suggested.

Mark frowned. 'Is that the earliest he can see me? I was under the impression that he wanted to get our deal sorted out now as a matter of urgency.'

'I'm sorry, Mr Barber. He's pretty tied up between now and — '

'Is he there?' Mark cut in. 'Could I have a word with him?'

'Well, he *is* rather busy — '

'So am I,' Mark replied. 'But what I have to say won't take a moment.'

After a while the secretary agreed to see if Mackenzie could spare him a few moments. At last Mackenzie's sandpaper voice came on the line.

'All right, Barber. What is it now?'

Mark smiled across at Laura, but no hint of the smile found its way into his voice. 'We had an appointment today. You broke it, twice. Now I understand that you can't see me again until the second week in January.'

'So?'

'I was under the impression you wanted this meeting today as a matter of urgency.'

Mackenzie made a sound in his throat. 'Something came up. It happens that way. Now, I think you'd better talk to me when you're not quite so emotional. Goodbye.'

'Just a moment, Mr Mackenzie. I only have one other thing to say.'

'Go on, then. But I'd be glad if you could make it quick.'

Laura watched Mark closely, wondering what on earth was coming next.

'Just before we rang off earlier, you told me not to forget a pen, because you might decide to sign an agreement here and now. Well, I fetched a pen, a very *special* pen.' He took from his pocket the black and gold fountain pen that Laura had bought him back in

July and held it up so that he could examine it. 'But since we're not going to use it today, I think we'd better just cancel whatever dealings we thought we were going to have altogether, don't you?'

'*What?* Do you know what you're say — '

'Well, look at it this way, Mr Mackenzie. Nine or ten months ago I told you I was interested in handling the New Shepham properties, but you kept me waiting right until today to arrange a meeting. Now you say you can't see me until the New Year. I'm sorry, but the fact is, I'm just not prepared to wait any longer.'

'But . . . Are you mad? I mean, do you know how much money you're turning away? Not to mention the prestige of being involved with Mackenzie Holdings?'

'Yes, I am. But I daresay we'll survive without you. Goodbye, Mr Mackenzie, and I hope you have a very merry Christmas.'

189

Laura watched him through surprised eyes. Her voice was hushed. 'Mark — what on earth have you done?'

He looked at her and smiled. 'I've just done the one thing I've wanted to do to that man for months, now — say 'no'.'

'But your father — '

' — isn't running Barber and Jennings any more. *I* am. And while I love him dearly and respect and value his opinions, the final decision must rest with me.'

'He isn't going to like it, you know.'

'I don't suppose he is. But that's my problem, not yours. Anyway, if we're lucky, Mackenzie will have a change of heart and come crawling back. I've offered him darn' good terms, and he knows it. He won't get a deal like this anywhere else.'

He glanced at his wristwatch, then pulled his seat-belt across his chest. 'Now — let's get back to Shepham. We've got some celebrating to do. Bill Everett's been a father for three whole hours, and we haven't even wet the baby's head yet!'

★ ★ ★

On the way back to the office they bought a bottle of champagne, and when they finally arrived at four-fifteen Laura, Mark and Trevor Teale took great pleasure in toasting baby and parents.

Some little while later Mark disappeared into his office, where he phoned his father to tell him what had happened with regard to the Mackenzie deal. When he came back out, Laura asked him how Derek had taken it.

'About as well as I expected,' Mark replied, in low spirits. 'Badly. But that can't be helped. It's over and done with now. And anyway, this is supposed to be a celebration!'

The champagne had a pleasantly numbing effect on all of them, and when they closed up at five o'clock,

Laura strolled home slowly, enjoying the feel of breezy night air reviving her.

Soon she was within sight of her cottage — and that was when she got the uneasy feeling that she was being followed.

She glanced over her shoulder, but gently-sloping Larkfield Lane appeared empty. Still, the feeling that she was not alone persisted.

As soon as she got inside the cottage she locked and bolted the front door, then unbuttoned her jacket and set down her shoulder bag. That nasty, flesh-creeping feeling of being watched had shattered the champagne-induced euphoria of mere moments before, and now Laura found herself frowning in worry that Keith had thrown caution to the wind and come back for her after all.

She decided to keep her mobile phone close, just in case.

But maybe it was just her imagination. After all, it had been a trying day. She was wound up and confused over what to think about Mark. Perhaps a shower and an early night —

Click!

She froze, standing in the centre of the darkened living room. She had heard a noise from somewhere outside, she was sure she had. But what was it? A cat, perhaps? Or *Keith?*

She strained her ears but caught no further sounds. Still . . . As quietly as she could she moved into the shadowy kitchen, intent on doing some careful checking — and was just in time to see a silhouette pass by the kitchen window.

So there *was* someone out there! The breath caught in her throat as she stood frozen in alarm.

She looked at the phone in her hand. She had to call Mark, get help. There was no telling what a man like Keith might do if pushed too far —

Again she jumped, for now she could see the silhouette against the kitchen door, and hear the sounds he made as he twisted the doorknob.

He was trying to get in!

But then, suddenly, the noise stopped, and the silhouette appeared almost to shrug. She heard a noise she couldn't identify. Then the figure disappeared from view. She heard a dull thud, as if something heavy had dropped, or fallen.

Then she heard a single muffled word.

' . . . help . . . '

She frowned. What was going on? Was this some kind of ruse to get her to unlock the door? She stood framed in the kitchen doorway, a picture of indecision. Then:

'Laura . . . please, it's . . . help . . . '

She couldn't tell whether it was a trick or not. It certainly *sounded* convincing. And if it *was* genuine, she couldn't wait any longer. Someone out there needed aid.

She crossed the kitchen until she reached the door. There, she pressed her face close to the window, misting the pane with her breath, searching in vain for some figure lurking in the dark side-alley.

' . . . please . . . '

The voice was quite clearly in pain.

There was nothing for it: she had to take a chance. She fumbled at the lock, twisted the handle and opened the door.

A wave of frigid air struck her like a blow and pushed her back a pace. She came forward again, looked out into the alley, but saw no-one.

' . . . ah . . . '

Then she looked down at the man lying at her feet and a small cry escaped her.

' . . . Laura . . . heart . . . '

It was Derek Barber.

★   ★   ★

There was no time for questions. Curiosity would have to wait. She knelt beside him and turned him gently onto his side. In the bright moonlight he looked old and close to death. His eyes slowly turned to her but he didn't appear to know who she was anymore. His face was screwed up in pain. He

croaked, 'Tablets . . . po . . . pocket
. . . coat pocket . . . '

Quickly she felt in the pocket of his
grey overcoat. Empty. As gently as she
could she rolled him onto his back and
felt in the other pocket. Her trembling
hand brought out a small container. She
took off the lid, tipped one small white
tablet into her palm and then, with her
free hand, lifted his head a little.

He seemed to be sinking fast.

'*Uncle Derek!* Stay with me, now!
Listen to me. Open your mouth. *Open
— your — mouth*. I'm going to slip a
table under your tongue.'

' . . . who . . . ?'

'You must do as I say!'

Sluggishly he obeyed her and she got
the tablet into his mouth.

'Now lie still. That's right. I'm not
going to leave you. Here, I'm going to
cover you with my jacket, and keep you
warm. Then I'll phone for an ambu-
lance.'

He frowned. ' . . . Laura? Is that
you . . . ?'

'Yes. Just lie still. I've got you now.'

And as she held him close she keyed three digits into the phone in her free hand.

999.

★ ★ ★

The hospital waiting room had plain, cream-coloured walls, and apart from a few public information posters and a print of Van Gogh's *Sunflowers*, there wasn't much to look at.

Laura and Mark sat in silence, waiting.

In the corridor outside they could hear the sounds of the hospital at work: echoing Tannoy announcements, the laughter and good-natured banter of the staff, the clanking of trolleys being wheeled from ward to ward and a regular flow of passing footsteps.

At last Mark looked up. His face was pale and there were tired circles beneath his eyes. She watched him shrug, then shake his head. 'What I don't understand is, what was he doing outside your cottage in the first place?' he asked.

She looked at him.

'Mum said that he'd been in a mood all day, but after he got my phone call he went and locked himself in his study. Half an hour later she found him in the hallway, putting his coat on. He told her he was going for a walk. But why did he come to *you?*'

She ran her moist eyes over his worried face. 'I don't know, Mark. I don't know.'

They continued to wait. The wall-clock read 8:31.

At 8:46 they heard footsteps approaching and both sat up expectantly. A moment later the door opened and Shirley Barber came in, looking as pale as her son. Her hair was in disarray and her eyes were red and sore where she'd been crying.

'Mum — ?' Mark could not bring himself to ask the question.

Shirley came further into the room and took a seat between them. Her movements were slow and obviously exhausted.

'His condition has stabilised,' she said quietly. At once fresh tears filled Laura's already scratchy eyes. 'He's still in intensive care, but the doctors say he'll live. Thank God. It's going to take him a long while to get over it, but — '

Mark sagged a little, and almost without realising it Laura reached out to take his hands in hers. Shirley, seeing the gesture, smiled tremulously.

'Did you speak to him?' Mark asked. 'I mean, did he say anything — '

His mother's tired nod silenced him. 'Yes, we did talk, for a while. Then he drifted off to sleep.'

Somewhere in the distance they heard a lonely two-tone siren wailing sadly.

'Did he say what he was going at Laura's place?'

Again Shirley nodded. 'Yes, he did.' She looked from one of them to the other, then drew herself up as if she had just reached a decision. 'Laura, I want to apologise to you in advance if some of what I'm going to say now upsets you. And Mark — although I'll understand it if you get angry, I want you to remember that your father only did what he thought was best for you — however difficult that may appear now.'

Mark felt the weight of Laura's hands on his. 'All right,' he said warily. 'We're listening.'

Shirley sniffed into a tightly-rolled paper handkerchief, composing herself. 'Your father has always been proud of you, Mark, of your own personal achievements as well as what you've done for Barber and Jennings, and I suppose for that reason he's always been a bit over-protective towards you.

'Although you're probably not aware of it, you're a very eligible young man. You're successful and you run your own highly profitable business. It sounds old-fashioned, I know, but you'd make a good catch for any girl.

'That's why it was always your

father's hope that when the time came for you to get married and settle down, your wife would be as supportive to you as, well, as I was to *him*, I suppose.'

Mark's frown could be heard in his voice. 'I don't understand. Where is all this leading?'

'Perhaps I'm not making a very good job of explaining things,' Shirley said uncomfortably. She fell silent for a moment as she tried to bring order to her words. Then: 'What I'm trying to say is this — that your father and I have known for some time how you feel about Laura, here. I sometimes think we knew even before *you* did.'

Mark stiffened in surprise.

'And while it would have been my dearest wish to see the two of you fall in love and get married,' Shirley continued, 'your father had very *different* ideas.'

She turned her kindly gaze to Laura. 'Derek has certain views on what Mark should look for in a woman. If he'd had his way, Mark would have ended up with a personal assistant-cum-secretary rather than a wife.'

Laura's face was slack with surprise at the revelation. 'I don't understand,' she whispered.

'No, but I do,' Mark cut in. 'At least I *think* I do.' He eyed his mother keenly. 'Because Dad didn't approve of Laura, he deliberately tried to match-make me with Sarah Clarke, didn't he? *She* was his idea of the perfect partner.'

Shirley inclined her head, ashamed. 'And when you rang him this afternoon and told him that the Mackenzie deal was off, he was furious. All along he had been convinced that Laura would distract you from the business, and now — at least to *his* way of thinking — he had proof that he'd been right. So . . . ' She faltered. 'So, according to what he just told me, he decided to . . . to try and *scare* Laura away from Shepham forever.'

'*What?*'

'Oh, he can see what a cruel and devious idea it was for himself, now,'

202

Shirley went on. 'He can't apologise enough. But he reasoned that if he made Laura believe that this Keith fellow had returned to launch some kind of vendetta against her, she might well decide to move away.'

'So he came to Laura's house tonight to begin his little campaign of terror,' Mark said in disgust. 'Mum, he must have been crazy — '

'Please, Mark. I know how angry you must feel, but believe me, your father's not entirely to blame. I've had a long talk with the doctors, and they think there may have been a mistake in his medication. Apparently, too much or too little can result in paranoia. And if you think about it, he was perfectly all right until he had his first heart attack two years ago. It was only *after* he was put on medication that he began to change.'

Mark glanced at Laura. She said softly, 'Your mother's right, Mark.'

Shirley added, 'Your father's a changed man now, Mark. He feels absolutely wretched that such a plan should ever have entered his head, especially in view of the fact that Laura here ended up saving his life when all his self-made aggravation triggered a heart attack. He'll never be able to thank you enough, Laura — and neither will I.'

The older woman rose from her chair and looked down at them. 'I . . . I think I'll go back into the ward now and sit with him for a while.'

Mark nodded. 'All right, Mum. We'll be right here if you need us.'

He and Laura rose to hug her. The moment was heavy with sentiment, a family reaffirming its love and support.

Back in the doorway again, Shirley scanned their faces closely. She felt in some strange way that a weight had been lifted from all three of them. 'It's going to take him a long time to get over tonight,' she said huskily. 'He'll need love and care and understanding if he's going to make it.'

Mark felt Laura's hand tighten on his

and smiled confidently. 'He'll get all three,' he reassured his mother. 'I promise.'

When they were alone again Mark turned to face Laura and smiled ruefully. He could not stand on ceremony any longer. He was just too tired to carry on pretending.

'She was right,' he said gently. 'I *do* love you, Laura. I'm sorry if that upsets you, or spoils our relationship in any way. But I can't help it. I've loved you for a long time now. In fact, now that I really *think* about it, I can't remember a time when I didn't.'

She looked up into his face with her shining eyes full of wonder.

'It's all right,' he added 'I understand if — '

She murmured something, and he froze.

'What?'

'I love you too,' she repeated.

He didn't appear to understand at first exactly what she had said. Then a joyful flush of warmth washed across his face, chasing the tiredness away, and his eyes mirrored the wonder in hers. 'You . . . that's . . . ' He shook his head, smiling. 'I don't know what to say!'

As their fingers entwined and their faces drew ever closer for the first real kiss of their new life together, she said softly, 'Then don't *say* anything.'

Their lips met, pressed firmly, lovingly together.

It had been an eventful five months, and the road they had travelled to reach this moment had not been without its hardships. But the journey had eventually given them each other — and that alone made it all worthwhile.

THE END

*Other titles in the
Linford Romance Library:*

DEAR OBSESSION

I. M. Fresson

Dr. Manley's wife Kate has allowed her son Johnnie to become an obsession, excluding the rest of her family. However, when the doctor takes a new partner, Dr. Paul Quest, everything changes. Johnnie becomes more independent and her husband less willing to go along with her obsession. Kate, now realising that she is in danger of losing her husband, must also accept the bitter truth: that Johnnie is capable of doing without her . . .